PRAI

"This is a gripping, intense story of loyalty and betrayal, against a vivid backdrop of an interstellar rebellion through labour solidarity. I can't wait to see what Palumbo writes next!"

— MARTHA WELLS, bestselling author of
The Murderbot Diaries and *Witch King*

"Furiously compelling. Palumbo paints her star-spanning universe and its cast with fluid, natural strokes, then jams a meteor between imperial teeth and dares them to bite. A harrowing space opera journey of injustice and revenge worth every tensed nerve and desperate hope."

— HAILEY PIPER, Bram Stoker Award-winning
author of *Queen of Teeth*

"I love Suzan Palumbo's short fiction, so when I heard she had a novella, I jumped at the chance to read it. *Countess* is a space adventure that maintains the hurtling energy of a pulp while highlighting the cultural complexity of diaspora and empire, the cruelty of a colonial future, and the bite of injustice. Grab it!"

— DEREK KÜNSKEN, author of *The Quantum Magician*
and *The House of Styx*

"Palumbo has woven a richly textured, beautifully complex tapestry of betrayal, anger, and revenge. The keen edge of justified rage against colonization and colonizers is wielded with great skill in this dark, intense retelling."

— PREMEE MOHAMED, World Fantasy and
Nebula Award-winning author

# PRAISE FOR *SKIN THIEF: STORIES*

"Palumbo proves masterful at taking material from folk-lore and making it personal, letting those things that are meant to terrify speak for themselves. Readers are sure to be impressed."

— *Publishers Weekly*

"If you like dark, literary, thought-provoking fiction, make this book your next read."

— ARLEY SORG for *Lightspeed*

"A triumphant collection of stories, ranging from dark fantasy to horror, exploring identity, oppression, and queerness. It is a collection of gothic delights, hauntings, Trinidadian folklore, and heartbreak."

— LYNDSIE MANUSOS for *Book Riot*

"The stories are dark and haunting and lavishly queer. Palumbo mines her Trinidadian and Canadian/Western heritages alike, blending her experiences together in a way that is both speculative and rooted in what feels like truth. Palumbo always leaves me feeling unmoored and prickly, thrilled and frightened. Readers new to her work and returning fans will each find things to love about this collection. There are no weak stories in the bunch."

— ALEX BROWN for *Locus*

# COUNTESS

SUZAN PALUMBO

Published by ECW Press
665 Gerrard Street East
Toronto, Ontario, Canada M4M 1Y2
416-694-3348 / info@ecwpress.com

Editor for the press: Jen Albert
Copy-editor: A.G.A. Wilmot
Cover art: Matt Griffin
Cover design: Jessica Albert

This is a work of fiction. Names, characters, places and incidents are the product of the author's imagination or are used fictitiously.

LIBRARY AND ARCHIVES CANADA CATALOGUING
IN PUBLICATION

Title: Countess / Suzan Palumbo.

Names: Palumbo, Suzan, author.

Identifiers: Canadiana (print) 20240365259 | Canadiana (ebook) 20240365267

ISBN 978-1-77041-757-1 (softcover)
ISBN 978-1-77852-302-1 (ePub)
ISBN 978-1-77852-305-2 (PDF)

Subjects: LCGFT: Science fiction. | LCGFT: Novels.

Classification: LCC PS8631.A49 C68 2024 | DDC C813/.6—dc23

This book is funded in part by the Government of Canada. Ce livre est financé en partie par le gouvernement du Canada. We acknowledge the support of the Canada Council for the Arts. Nous remercions le Conseil des arts du Canada de son soutien. We would like to acknowledge the funding support of the Ontario Arts Council (OAC) and the Government of Ontario for their support. We also acknowledge the support of the Government of Ontario through the Ontario Book Publishing Tax Credit, and through Ontario Creates.

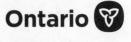

PRINTED AND BOUND IN CANADA          PRINTING: FRIESENS     5   4   3   2   1

For J, J, and A

*There is horror here,*
*but there is also always hope.*

# ONE

# INVICTA

Acting Captain Virika Sameroo abandoned her seat and stood ramrod stiff behind the *Oestra's* navigator after it jolted through the Invictan region skip gate.

Invicta, the ruby- and sapphire-hued capital planet of the Æcerbot Empire floating in the ink void of space before them, had always compelled her to her feet, even as a hollow-cheeked child staring out of the porthole of the immigrant ship *Zarak* two decades earlier. Her heart lifted like a balloon filled with hope as she watched her naturalized home grow larger on the screen. She resisted the urge to place her right hand on her chest in homage. Instead, she held her chin high and kept her face as implacable as ice.

*Success or perish*, she repeated inwardly. The mantra had been a touchstone, a beacon throughout her darkest merchant fleet academy days. It had spurred her onward in spite of exhaustion, loneliness, and the whispered slurs hurled at her by her fellow recruits denigrating her brown skin and Exterran Antillean heritage. She'd survived the academy, and she would see the *Oestra's* mission through now.

"Med bay?" She spoke into the armrest com on the captain's chair, her voice as cool as her expression.

"Yes, Lieuten— Captain?" The stumble over her rank stabbed her. Heat crept up her throat and along the edges of her jaw.

"Status report on Captain Whitehall?"

"He's conscious. Weak as a polar fawn, but stable, Captain Sameroo."

"Do all you can for him." She was unable to smooth the crimp of concern in her tone. Images of Captain Whitehall flooded her mind: the captain soaking in acrid sweat, writhing in an indomitable fever, confusion flashing in his unfocused eyes. She'd die before she failed to bring Captain Whitehall, the man she'd come to think of as a surrogate father, back to Invicta alive. Her love for him was the one emotion she refused to douse. She tensed and cocked her head left at the acting second-in-command seated in front of the communication com. "Lieutenant Lyric?"

"Crew's ready and in preparation for docking and disembarkation." Lyric kept his gaze on the touch console in front of him, his square jaw set. He refused to look at her. If she compelled eye contact with him now, she'd be met with a defiant, open-dagger stare that he was no longer able to mask.

"Excellent." The word rose up from her diaphragm, resonating lower than her natural speaking voice. She'd used the same register before twice with Lyric. Once, a year and a half earlier, when he'd put his clammy hand on her inner thigh in the officers mess after they'd both been promoted to lieutenant. The other only days ago, in the ship's conference room, when she'd shut down his demand for shared command of the *Oestra* after Whitehall had fallen ill with the fevers.

"We're both lieutenants. We're equals," he'd growled and pounded the table with his sizable fist. His face had gone as crimson as Invictan Lorryberry trees when he realized she would not relinquish any of her command to him.

"The captain left explicit instructions for me to assume the helm. He trusted *me*." She'd held Lyric's gaze, refused to give him the satisfaction of agreeing they were equal in any way in the chain of authority. He would steamroll her flat if she deferred to him. The rebuff had compelled him into discipline, but it had not extinguished his disdain. It emanated towards her and filled the bridge. She'd shouldered his burgeoning insubordination since they'd departed Icacos in the neutral transport zone shared by Æcerbot, Kaspan, and some smaller powers with their coveted iridium shipment.

Hands at her sides, she remained outwardly stoic for the remainder of the journey, never daring to let a trace of the mire of fatigue and worry bubbling inside her break her demeanour. Any slip in judgement or confidence would slither its way from Lyric's tongue to her superiors, and she would bear the stinging account of it.

She trembled only once during planetary approach, letting her mind wander through the cramped rooms of her mother's apartment in Paria, on the outskirts of Elmet, Invicta's capital city. Her tongue involuntarily curled around the ghost of the pepper stew her mother had prepared for dinner the night before the *Oestra* shipped out. Ma had started trembling when Virika told her they'd be transporting iridium.

"What if yuh get raided?" Her mother spoke around a sob lodged in her throat. "Dem dam privateer and dem go cut yuh throats and kill yuh." She wrung her hands. "I can't lose yuh, too." Tears dripped down her face.

"You won't lose me, Ma," Virika said with her fists balled as hard as steel. "No one will take me from you, I promise." That promise had been a gamble. The privateer raids that Æcerbot officials suspected were funded in part by the Kaspans had become more frequent and bloody over the last year. Privately, she worried, but standing at the helm, Virika exuded confidence. She *would* bring everyone home safe. Invicta would have her iridium shipment. Captain Whitehall would get the care he needed, and she would wipe her mother's tears while sitting across from her at their dinner table.

She let herself smile a little, rolling the memory of the pepper stew around her tongue, allowing it to morph gradually into an ache for Alba's full lips. She caught herself mid-shiver and re-steeled herself for the task at hand. Soon, they'd dock in Invicta's golden capital, and she'd be able to breathe again.

Twenty-four hours later, Virika and the crew were met by Commander Everbrook and Military Attaché Andilet, who were dressed in their formal blue-and-red attire at the Elmet base. She saluted Captain Whitehall as he was transferred from the *Oestra* to the base hospital for tests and treatment. He did not respond. Her heart cracked. Whitehall's fever had spiked again hours before arrival, inducing hallucinations.

"Vultures! Kaspan Vultures," he'd screamed. He insisted he was being eaten alive. She'd signed off on the sedation to stop him from ranting and clawing his face bloody. The anguish frozen on his gouged, unconscious brow wounded her as they wheeled him away.

"We trust Captain Whitehall's full medical report along with your observations of the events leading up to his . . . removal from duty are included in your log and files." Attaché Andilet's glare bored into her as he spoke. His voice, like his face, was as smooth as cream. Virika recognized the latent curdle of scorn in his eyes.

"Well done, Lieutenant." Commander Everbrook clapped his fleshy hands. "That iridium's got to be processed and sent off to the building docks immediately. Privateers 'round skip gates have intercepted too much of it already. It's a miracle they didn't target you."

The three watched as the heavy cargo was unloaded. Virika stood slightly apart from her superiors. Outwardly, her joints and spine were made of iron; within her, a sliver of the child she'd been on the immigrant ship quivered.

The immigrant labour ship *Zarak* had been stifling. One baby or another screamed the entire voyage. Utilitarian food and drink were rationed at scheduled times. There'd been long stretches during the trip when hunger scraped Virika's stomach. All the immigrant passengers had left their homes and families on Orinoco in the Exterran Antilles for the chance to escape the punishing mining life after winning the immigration lottery. If Virika's family had stayed, the gruelling work would have eroded her father's lungs and killed him. The dust cut the lifespan of everyone living near the mines by a third compared to those who lived on Invicta. Still, as a girl, she could not see how leaving would lead to a better life.

"I don't want to go. I don't want to leave my friends," she'd cried as they boarded the ship. Every jostle through the skip gates from the Exterran Antilles into the neutral zone and out into Æcerbot territory had made her nauseous. Her father placed his calloused miner's hand on her cheek to reassure her. He'd always seen straight through to the source of her troubles.

"Virika means bravery," he'd said.

Now, she'd become the first Exterran Antillean to ever helm an Æcerbot ship. She wished her father were alive to see it. The gravity of the moment, the historicity of her within it, wound the remnant of the little girl inside her tight.

She marked the occasion in silence.

When the last of the cargo and crew had been accounted for, she was dismissed by Commander Everbrook and Attaché Andilet with a salute. She moved through the massive gleaming granite base offices and corridors, filling out logs and initialling waybills — keeping strict Invictan standards as she had her entire life, the whispered hopes of her parents and her people at the back of her mind, driving her forward.

Alone in her sleek base apartment, a ten-minute walk from the main headquarters block, Virika placed her bag on her bed and unpacked the few personal effects she'd brought with her off planet: a faded picture of her parents on Orinoco from before she was born — her father's lean jaw determined, the tug of fear pulling at the corners of her mother's mouth; a worn book of Tagore poetry annotated by both her and Alba; and the emerald green dragon-shaped lapel pin she'd received when she enlisted.

She pulled a white cotton packet from the satchel in her duffle bag. The scent of cardamom and cloves diffused throughout the room. She inhaled and was back in the colourful open-air market outside the dock city of Icacos, enveloped in the voices of merchants from across Exterran space hawking their wares. The scorching Icacos midday sun had driven Virika to the market in search of refreshment often. One afternoon, she'd come across a stall piled high with plump Exterran Antillean fruit. She tested the ripeness of a Tollian Julie mango between her thumb and index finger and then noticed the vendor. The old woman's eyes were dark and sharp, taking in Virika's tan uniform. A slant of distrust marked her mouth.

"They sweet?" Virika asked the old woman. She winked as she gestured at the mangoes with her chin. The woman's suspicion faded into a smirk. She was about Virika's mother's age, her skin a deep brown and her hair plaited into a long, thick salt-and-pepper braid down her back.

"Sweeta den anything yuh eva had." The woman's eyes twinkled.

Virika laughed. "I'll take two!" She handed the woman a sovereign. "Keep the change," she said, slipping the fruit into her satchel.

"Soldier." Virika glanced up, a smile budding in anticipation of what mischief the woman might say. "Take dis for dee extra money. Go on." The woman handed Virika the small cotton packet marked with what appeared to be an old Devanagari-style script.

"What is it?" Virika asked. "A tea?"

"Ah charm. Don't drink it, yuh hear? Keep it with yuh. It does cut blight."

Virika considered the packet in her hand. Her parents had sworn to renounce the vestiges of the old practices to migrate from the Exterran Antilles to Invicta. It had been a required part of their immigration lottery application.

At home in the capital, such an object would be confiscated, its bearer punished by a hefty fine. The Æcerbot Empire and its ceremonial emperor were God himself; they tolerated none other. Yet here in neutral space, and off at the fringe mining sectors where she'd been born, the old ways lingered. She looked at the woman and saw her own mother alone in her tiny kitchen, eating dinner at an empty table, counting the days until Virika's return. Virika would humour this old woman as she hoped someone from the Paria neighbourhood was at that moment humouring her mother and listening to her long-winded stories. She'd get rid of the packet before she shipped off to Invicta.

"Thank you." She bowed her head and continued her walk through the bustling market, filling her sack with dried fruit and a soft purple Anduvian wool scarf. She revisited the woman's stall to talk to her the following day, again imagining that someone light years away was visiting her own mother. But the stall was empty.

"The Baroness is only at the market twice a week," the man who'd sold her the scarf explained.

"Is that her name?" Virika found herself grinning.

"It's what she calls herself," the man laughed.

The *Oestra* shipped out before Virika could say goodbye to the Baroness.

Virika inhaled the sachet's spicy scent once more. She hadn't intended to bring the packet back to Invicta. It served no purpose here. Yet she couldn't bring herself to throw the old woman's "blessing" in the chute. She placed the packet on her dresser, next to the picture of her mother and father she'd unpacked earlier.

Next, she took out an iridium and copper alloy coin, three millimetres thick and thirty millimetres in diameter. A pelican was struck on one face, the words "to dwell in unity" on the other — the emblem and motto of Toussard's failed rebellion on the planet Bequia, crushed more than a decade before. The privateers that trolled the neutral and border spaces of the Exterran empires pillaging ships had adopted the symbol to signify their independence from any governing body. Under her apartment's overhead lights, the tiny amount of iridium in the coin made it shimmer like a butterfly wing in the sun. Iridium was solid, unbreakable, and the anchor of the Æcerbot Empire. Their ships, the skip gates — all of it required a heat-protective coating of iridium to function. Æcerbot was in constant competition over control of its extraction and price with the Kaspan Empire and other smaller powers. Virika had never held a coin partly made from it before; it was too precious to Æcerbot, too critical to the functioning of interplanetary transport and trade, which were the lifeblood of the empire's economy. She would give the coin to her mother if there were a way it could be spent without suspicion. As it was, it was as useful as an ornament. She placed it in a box on the dresser next to her dragon pin as a reminder of her unwavering oath, pushing the distaste of how the coin had come into her possession from her mind.

After she'd tidied her space, stowing her luggage under her bed and decluttering her dresser, she ran herself a hot shower. Only once she'd slipped out of her uniform did she feel the cares of the mission fall from her. The sudden lightness made her dizzy; she braced herself against the shower wall to keep from fainting. When she stepped under the stream of water, letting it hit the back of her neck, the remaining burdens of the last five weeks sluiced from her shoulders. Alone at last, she could not stop herself from crying.

# TWO

# REUNION

Captain Whitehall's room was on the third floor of the Elmet base medical complex. Two days after their return, Virika was granted permission to visit him, though Whitehall's attending physicians warned her that the Icacos mosquito-borne fever he'd contracted had diminished his cognitive abilities. She fortified herself as she navigated the state-of-the-art complex, battering down memories of arriving at a dingy city hospital in her parents' suburb of Paria to identify her father's mangled body. She'd gone rigid when she'd gotten the call that her father had been crushed in an air dock accident. Her stomach burned now as it did then. The astringent hospital scent would forever be a harbinger of death for her.

She owed her promotion to first lieutenant to Captain Whitehall. He'd fought for her when the board had only wanted Lyric as lieutenant on the *Oestra*.

"Lyric is the lazy son of a rich former minister. He's competent, but he's gotten further faster because of who his father knows," Captain Whitehall had argued in front of the board. Lyric had turned bright red. He'd rebuffed

Virika afterwards when she'd asked him how he felt about her being assigned to the post as well.

She stifled her thoughts of Lyric as she reached Whitehall's door. She opened it, held her breath, and stepped inside.

The dim room was silent except for the beeps and whirs of the monitors tracking Whitehall's vitals. They were a solemn, metronomic reminder of his tenuous condition. The fever had chewed away at the robust captain quickly, much quicker than was typical according to the doctors on Icacos and here on base. He'd been a ruddy wall of a man when they'd left Invicta, with a handshake that compelled you to acknowledge his authority. Now, with his concave cheeks and grey varicose skin, the spectre of death had already claimed dominion over him. She pulled a chair close to his bed. His flaky eyelids fluttered open at the sound. His unfocused milky gaze, so unlike the bright, alert one she'd known, settled on her.

"Vulture . . ." his sandpaper voice rasped and his dry throat clicked like a machine needing oil. Virika winced. He was worse.

"Captain." She managed a smile. "How are you? We're eager for your return to command." She spoke encouragingly, though the hope of him ever resuming his post was shrivelling within her.

"Who was the vulture?" he continued, oblivious to her question. His clouded violet eyes pinned her to her seat.

"There was no vulture, Captain." The corner of her mouth twitched. He was not himself.

"LIAR!" His voice ground like seizing gears. His desiccated lips puckered and cracked. Blood began to drip down the side of his face. He tried to spit on her but only managed to spatter his chin with blood. Virika pushed her chair away, repulsed by the living corpse who'd mentored her like a parent. She stood, her face alight with shame.

"Sir. You'd contracted the fever on Icac—"

"Shut up, you ungrateful coolie bitch!"

Virika flinched as if struck. Though she'd been called the word in whispers at the academy, the slur was rarely spoken openly or out loud. Whitehall shifted, grasping at her. He lost his balance and crashed to the floor, on his side. Cords ripped from his arms. The monitors sent alarms screeching throughout the room and the halls outside. He shrieked like a wounded animal. Virika made for the door, thinking only of alerting the staff and aiding the captain. Two orderlies and a physician burst inside. They blocked her view of Whitehall as they tended to him.

"You'll have to leave, Lieutenant," a nurse said, pushing past Virika and brushing her out of the room.

The door slammed shut in her face. She stood, her mind reeling, feeling heartbroken. *Coolie.* He saw her like the others did, an unwanted, dirty immigrant. *No, no. He's been too supportive of me. Too helpful. He's sick. He can't think clearly. This is not my captain. He'll get better.* Virika looked down. She was twisting the hem of her uniform in her hands while the remaining medical staff on duty watched. She spun on her heel and headed towards the exit.

On base that evening, Virika walked to the administrative block apartments. The late summer sun was setting. The sky was a brilliant orange and there was a frisson mounting within her that electrified the air. She'd anticipated this reunion more than any other. The memory of how she'd met Alba two years ago replaced the painful image of Whitehall's suffering and made her break out into a jog. They'd collided with each other on the steps of the Strategic Planning Building. Alba had been hurrying out, carrying a box of her things to her new office at the Ministry of Trade.

"I'm sorry," Virika said, concern wrinkling her brow over whether she'd hurt the slighter woman. "I—"

"I know who you are. I've been following your career. We have a lot in common, Virika," Alba had said as she smiled and dusted herself off. Virika found herself raising an eyebrow and smiling back, intrigued by the idea that she might have something in common with this attractive woman.

"Have a drink with me. I can apologize properly for knocking into you, and you can show me how much we're alike," Virika said after she'd helped Alba pick up her belongings.

Drinks had turned into an evening of Alba describing her childhood in a fishing village in the remote province of Tinian, where she'd been raised by her widowed father. They'd both had the same working-class upward struggle. By the end of that first date, Virika knew she was in danger of falling for Alba, who, despite being Invictan, understood the pressures faced by a daughter trying to provide for her family. Alba was like no one she'd met before.

The lift in Alba's building took seconds to reach the twelfth floor. Virika exited and walked down the marble hall. Her heart thrummed as she knocked on the non-descript door.

"Hello," Alba said as she opened it. She was dressed in a black tunic and leggings. Her straight brown hair framed her high cheekbones and spilled about her shoulders. Virika could not suppress the smile forming on her lips. Alba pulled her inside her apartment and closed the door behind them. "Where have you been?" she asked with a wink that pushed Virika's knees to the brink of buckling.

"Oh, captaining an Æcerbot merchant ship." Virika feigned nonchalance by inspecting her nails.

"I heard! It was all over the Ministry of Trade and the base." Alba bounced. "Virika, that's —"

"That's Captain Virika, to you." She pulled a stern face and pointed a finger at Alba. Alba pouted before pressing Virika up against the door and kissing her so long and hard that Virika could focus on nothing except the unbridled desire tearing its way through her.

"Welcome home, Captain," Alba whispered when she eased away. She led Virika to the bedroom, where she kissed, and kissed, her everywhere until Virika was incoherent and shaking.

"Did you like commanding the ship?" Alba asked, her arm slung around Virika in bed. "Aside from being concerned for Whitehall."

"I did. Everything went as well as could be expected, except that Lyric couldn't stand that Whitehall made me captain. He was on the edge of open disgust and insubordination the entire journey home," Virika said, spent and lying with her head on Alba's shoulder. "If I were Invictan, he'd have accepted my authority."

Alba turned to look at Virika. "Or is it because you're a woman and he's from a rich family? That man thinks he's better than everyone. Calling him prejudiced when you were his captain will not endear you to the marine or win you any support." She touched Virika's cheek. Virika fought the urge to argue by changing the subject, as she often did when they broached this subject.

"I brought you a present," Virika said. She shifted off the bed and grabbed her pants.

"More gifts?" Alba laughed. "Wasn't *that* enough?" She smiled lazily. Virika lingered on the faint dimple on Alba's cheek. How lucky she was to have this gorgeous, brilliant trade strategist waiting to welcome her home.

She settled back next to Alba and fished something out of her pants pocket. "Open your hand," she ordered. Alba squinted, suspicious, and did as she was told. Virika placed the coin in the centre of Alba's palm. Alba pulled her hand towards herself to examine it closely. She went stone still.

"An-an iridium alloy coin? It's heavy!" She flipped it over and saw the pelican. The corners of her mouth slipped downward. "The rebellion?"

Virika put her own hands on her chest and watched as Alba shifted her palm to make the coin shimmer in the light.

"How'd you get it? I've never seen one before."

"Someone gave it to me."

Alba's mouth compressed. "It's dangerous to keep one of these. They gave it to you? No strings attached?"

"I wouldn't say that," Virika said. "I cut all the strings myself. It's a souvenir now, and it's mine." She closed Alba's hand around the coin. "I'm giving it to you."

"Me?" Disbelief shaded Alba's voice. She cocked her head.

Virika kissed Alba's hands. "I'd share everything I have with you." She shrugged. Alba studied Virika's face. The look in her eyes morphed from questioning to piercing concentration.

"You mean that, don't you?" Her cheeks coloured pink.

"I do," Virika said before leaning forward and kissing her.

"I'd give this to my father if I could." Alba bit her bottom lip for a moment. "But I'll keep it for you." She smiled as Virika covered her mouth with her lips.

The next morning, Virika took the light rail from her apartment to Elmet's gilded central station, which was packed with tourists from the outer provinces. Empire officials, in their tunics and bright sashes, as well as Invictan civilians bustling to places of business or pleasure filled the spacious grand halls. She'd changed into a white blouse and linen pants, the style of clothing favoured by Antillean immigrants, before she hopped on the connection to the west-end suburb of Paria, where she'd grown up. The image of the captain, helpless and broken on the floor, haunted her as she watched her fellow passengers' faces morph from the predominant pale Invictan heritage to the tans and deep browns of the Antillean immigrant neighbourhoods. The stations grew shabbier and the crimson Lorryberry trees farther apart the longer they travelled west. Soon, the gleaming white towers that housed the Invictan middle classes were replaced with haphazardly planned subdivisions.

Paria was the only place in Elmet where Virika could melt into the crowd. Everyone on the train now appeared to be of Antillean origin. Here she wasn't a lieutenant but the daughter of Kendon and Savitri Sameroo: the girl who moved up and got out, the one who'd draped herself in the iridescent Empire flag and swallowed Æcerbot doctrine. Paria was no longer her home, but she could still pretend. You could pretend yourself into being anyone if you threw your whole being into the act, she'd learned.

To Everbrook and Attaché Andilet, the success of her mission, her success in general, stemmed from the superiority of Invictan education. She'd delivered by conquering her flawed lineage, which could be traced from those mining and agricultural planets on the edges of the Empire all the way back centuries ago to the old British colonies on Terra. There, her people had once been enslaved and indentured to provide sugar for Andilet's and Everbrook's ancestors' tea. Space colonization had not been the great equalizer the capitalist billionaires had advertised. When their homes vanished due to the rising seas, the people of the Antillean islands found no sanctuary from any nation on Terra. With nowhere to go, they signed contracts that put them back into bondage, to work jobs on the far-flung mining and agricultural planets. Jobs those who chose to leave Terra willingly did not want. The Exterran Antilleans had self-government now but remained cowed in economic servitude to the Empire-based mining and agro-industrial corps. As it was on Terra, so it was in the Æcerbot Empire. Virika knew that the only way her family would survive would be for her to become a model Æcerbot citizen. Her success had proven she'd done it.

Exiting at the rundown Paria station, she walked to the apartment complex her family had lived in since they'd arrived in Elmet. Virika had offered to move her mother closer to the base, but her mother had refused to leave the memories of Virika's father, and their community, behind. The aroma of jerk chicken and pepper coming from Charlie's restaurant, which had occupied the same building since before her family arrived, filled the air.

"Ey, gyal!" he called and waved to her as she passed by.

She waved back. "I'm coming for some jerk chicken later!" she yelled. The same colourful signage and familiar faces greeted her from shop fronts she'd patronized most of her life. Nothing had changed in Paria in the five weeks that Virika had been gone. Only Virika knew she had come home a captain.

She entered the building and took the stairs to her mother's sixth-floor apartment rather than wait on the slow lift. Their good friend Audette lived in one of the apartments along the way. She'd have to remember to say hello to the kind woman later.

Pausing in front of her mother's door, Virika exhaled and then knocked.

Virika's mother flung the door open, reached out, and squeezed her as if she'd collapse if she let Virika go.

"Yuh ready to eat?" her mother asked when she released her. Virika studied her mother's face before answering.

Was it possible that her hair was greyer? That the sag of her skin on her lower neck was more pronounced, in such a short time? The sore guilt her mother always evoked in her when she had to leave Invicta throbbed. How would she handle Virika being commissioned as a captain in charge of longer, more dangerous assignments?

"Ready!" Virika's smile betrayed no sign of the turmoil she felt leaving Captain Whitehall's bedside, or her worries over Lyric. Her mother bolted the door behind them and they went to the kitchen. Virika sat in her chair at the metal table — the same table they'd eaten at since she was a girl. There followed an Exterran Antillean feast: buttery parathas daubed in tomato and eggplant chokas, fragrant with cumin, garlic, and cilantro. Savoury curried Invictan king fish seasoned with thyme, pepper, and lime, so tender it melted on your tongue. Chutneys, sweet and spicy to balance the full-bodied flavour of the sauces. The ship's mess could never hold a wooden pot spoon to her mother's cooking. Virika's throat grew thick as she watched her mother bustle around the kitchen.

"Ma, sit down. I haven't seen you in weeks."

"I will. I will. I want to make sure yuh belly is full." When she finally came to the table, her mother's portion was barely a quarter of what she'd served Virika.

"How have you been?" Virika paused between mouthfuls to ask.

Her mother's shoulders fell. They both avoided looking at the framed portrait Virika had sketched of her father that her mother kept on the counter. The insurance payout they'd paid monthly dues for barely covered his funeral. The fees to be cremated as a non-citizen immigrant had wiped out all their savings. They'd come to Invicta for the chance to give Virika citizenship and to a build better life. For that, Kendon Sameroo had paid with his life.

Virika recalled the day she told her mother she'd quit art school and enlisted in the fleet as a way to help support them both. The recruiters had approached her at the college. When they'd explained she'd be guaranteed a job, she could not in sound conscience say no.

"I will be everything they want me to be. I will put in extra time. I will never complain. I will work harder than any native-born recruit and they will not be able to deny that we are worthy. I will pass all their tests and they will see that we deserve to be here and that we are just like them."

"What if something happen to yuh? Who I go have?" Her mother's fear of losing her had been at the core of all of their arguments.

"We can't pay for me to go into the professions. I've told you." Irritation crept into her voice. "Not on your wages at the garment factory. How else can we eat, unless some Invictan family of means wants to adopt an Exterran Antillean teen-ager out of the goodness of their heart? There's no way for us to have any more than what we have now. The fleet will pay for my schooling. I'll be guaranteed a post on an airship. I'll make more than enough to send you money and take care of myself. Isn't that what we came here for in the first place? A better life? I mean look at this dump Dad died pay—"

Her mother slapped the rest of the words from her mouth. Virika tightened her jaw and put her hand to her stinging cheek.

"Yuh father dead so that yuh could come home and say yuh joining dee fleet, not for a dump. Don't let dese

29

people make yuh forget who yuh is, Viri." She shook her head. "What yuh think yuh woulda be back on Orinoco? Married to some man in dee mine. They did tell we people come colonize space with us. In dee Æcerbot Empire everybody is equal, and look what happen? We was back working again to make other people rich." She shook her head. "I sorry, I hit yuh."

"It's okay," Virika managed to say.

"Do what yuh want." The fire in her mother's voice had diminished to a smoulder that only reignited whenever Virika shipped out.

After dinner, Virika fell asleep in front of her mother's victascroll. She woke later to her mother hunched forward, watching a report of fresh Exterran Antillean privateering raids near skip gates in neutral zones connecting Æcerbot planetary territories in other solar systems with Æcerbot's main system. A suspicious peace existed between the empires in shared systems. Military presence and advanced technology were kept at a minimum for fear they would be used by one empire, especially Æcerbot, to encroach on another's territory. All skip gates let out from each star system into the neutral zone, to create a buffer that established nondirect cargo routes between empires. The Exterran Antilles star system consisting of three stars and just under a dozen habitable planets, all rich in resources, were not technically political colonies, though they were economically beholden to and subjugated by Æcerbot and the other empires' industries. They, too, were separated from the empires by a minimally patrolled neutral zone to maintain the pretence of their independence. All knew the empires would not hesitate to amass their military forces in the Exterran Antillean zones if they felt their commercial control over the planets were under serious threat. A handful of Exterran Antillean privateers had taken to exploiting the current loose security by raiding Æcerbot cargo ships, which the other empires conveniently let slide. The raids had been too scattered and sporadic throughout all of Exterran space for Æcerbot to effectively target and crush them.

Virika sat silently. Her mother muttered and held her head in her hands as the broadcasters detailed a recent raid.

"I shame dese are dee same people as we. Instead of working to get ahead, dese people thief and kill," she said. Virika thought back to the encounter she'd had with the privateer captain at the Gilded Lady pub on Icacos. Distaste soured her mouth.

"Ma," she said when the program ended. She'd avoided telling her mother about the journey home earlier; but she couldn't hide the situation from her indefinitely. "I was promoted to acting captain during the mission. Captain Whitehall picked up the fevers and I commanded the *Oestra* back to Invicta." Her mother sat up straight, fear cresting in her eyes.

"Did dey attack dee ship? Did yuh have to outrun dem like dese ships on dee news?" Her questions came fast, fuelled by rising panic. "Lord dis is why I didn't want yuh in dis job. Dey could have caught all yuh and kill every last one of yuh."

"No, Ma." Virika reached over and held her mother's hand. "The only trouble was Whitehall's illness. He is very sick, but he will pull through. I know he will . . ."

Her mother bowed her head wearily. Virika managed a reassuring smile.

"Okay, yuh know what yuh doing." She rubbed her forehead. "I sorry Whitehall get sick. He is a good man and helped yuh plenty. I hope he gets bettah."

"Me, too, Ma. I think I'll turn in." She took her mother's hands again and kissed them before standing up and heading to her childhood bedroom, with its walls covered in posters of art by Invictan artists she'd dreamed of emulating when she grew up.

"Lieutenant Sameroo!" A familiar voice summoned Virika from the hall outside her mother's apartment the next morning as they sat eating breakfast. The command was followed by a stern but even knock.

Her mother's face pinched with fear.

"One moment," Virika called.

She went to her room and slipped a black tunic over her sleeveless shirt. Her heart pounded. Her mind raced to Captain Whitehall's condition as she returned to the living room. Her mother opened the door. Military police flanked the threshold. Attaché Andilet stood in the centre of the hall.

"Yes, sir? Is everything all right?" Virika stepped forward to stand next to her mother.

"First Lieutenant Virika Sameroo, you are hereby charged with sedition, treason, and the murder of Captain Edmund Whitehall."

"Sedition? Murd—" her mother began before an officer pushed her aside while another grabbed Virika by the shoulders, his grip like a clamp. Yet another wrenched Virika's hands behind her back and zip-tied them.

"Murder? He's dead?" Virika's voice broke as all breath went out of her.

"You have the right to remain silent —" Andilet wasn't listening to her. Her head swam. She knew the required speech by rote. She'd learned the procedure when she took her oath of office aboard the *Oestra*. She'd been proud to take her part in the evitable clockwork of justice upholding Empire law.

"Virika, what's happening?" The terror in her mother's voice ripped through the rest of the commotion.

"Don't worry, Ma," she called out, not able to see what was happening behind her. "Stay calm. This is a misunder-standing." Her logs would prove it. She'd done everything she could for Whitehall. Would *still* do anything for h—. But Andilet had said the captain was dead. *Treason?* How had she been unloyal to her oath, to the Empire? She couldn't justify even thinking of it. *Go along with them. I'll sort this out. The Empire is just. I've come so far*, she thought.

Her mind flashed to the scene two days before, Captain Whitehall broken and bloody on the hospital floor, moni-tors screaming. Could it have been her visit that pushed him over the brink?

"Do you understand your rights, Lieutenant Sameroo?" the attaché asked, ignoring her question.

"I do." She swallowed in an attempt to remain composed.

"Excellent. Bates, Heath, secure the prisoner and come with me. The rest of you, search the apartment and question the neighbours. Document everything you find meticulously.

We don't want this case thrown out." The officer behind Virika shoved her forward. None of the residents who lived on the floor had dared step out into the hall, but Virika knew they were behind their doors listening and worrying for their own safety. She went without resistance, hoping that if she obeyed the officers no one would be hurt. Halfway down the hall, one of the men moved in close to her. His breath on the back of her neck made her hair stand on end.

"Savage slut," he whispered in a guttural voice then grabbed her behind. "Like being on the bottom, don't you, Captain? Does your mother like that, too?"

Virika's mind blanked. Rage splintered her restraint. She would bear the insults pointed at her. She would not tolerate them aimed at her mother. She whipped her head forward and then back, smashing her skull into his nose. "Fuck you," she spit out before she was knocked flat to the ground.

"Eight, Sixteen," Attaché Andilet yelled. Several officers pinned her down. They were crushing her chest. Claustrophobic panic screamed within her.

The pig she'd hit yelled, "Fuck that bitch." There was blood on the tiled floor. *Good*. She hoped she'd broken his face.

Attaché Andilet got down on his hands and knees and looked her in the eye.

"Sameroo, I know it's difficult for your kind to control itself, but do try. See, now we have to add resisting arrest and assault to that list of charges, and with all these witnesses they'll hardly be dropped." He stood up again. "Officer Heath, go attend to your face. The rest of you, keep a good

34

hold of her. We'll come back for the search after she's secured. Bates, take her mother in as well."

Virika's mother yelped as if she had been grabbed. The officers pushed Virika forward, preventing her from turning around and keeping distance from her head as they compelled her down the hall. There had to be someone to speak on her behalf. As soon as she could, she'd tell her lawyer to call Commander Everbrook. He'd always been kind and helpful. He'd listen to her. She recounted the *Oestra*'s personnel manifest. When she remembered that Lyric had cozied up to everyone aboard the ship, she was suddenly so tired she could no longer think. Her mother. Their friends. How could she protect them? Her legs collapsed under her. She did not attempt to right herself as the officers dragged her from the building.

## THREE

# INNOCENCE

Virika, dressed in an olive-coloured prison tunic, tensed in the witness stand. A dull ache pulsed in the centre of her forehead — the result of being questioned for two hours by the most patronizing prosecutor she'd ever met. He was the quintessential Æcerbot official — restrained and anally exacting. The part in his brown hair was so precise it looked as if he'd cut into his scalp with a razor. The sight of it made Virika wince. To her left, a broad-shouldered military judge wearing a navy robe presided behind an ornately carved desk. He was silent and austere. She commanded none of his sympathies.

Across from Virika, the five-member tribunal that would decide her fate stared her down. They were as unflinching as marble pillars. She recognized some of her jury from cere-monial inspections and various troopings of the colours. Dressed identically for the trial in their official grey tunics, she could not place their names or ranks. Did they recall her? They must know of her — she was one of the few commissioned Antillean officers in the merchant marine. At least a couple of the assembled had praised her precision and leadership during drills. Her record until this moment had been virtually impeccable. It had to be for her to have achieved lieutenancy so quickly.

She concentrated on the blue, ruby, and silver flag of the Empire hanging behind the tribunal box. It was her only comfort in the room. The closed military court did not allow civilian spectators. The prosecutor had argued that a trial against the first Exterran Antillean acting captain might provoke unrest in Paria. The stern judge had agreed and banned all reports of the proceedings. As she met the barrage of questions from the prosecutor now, she imagined the military police interrogating her mother. Had they hurt her? Virika was sick over not being able to see or talk with her. Her mother would surely be inconsolable over not being permitted to witness the tribunal.

Virika's counsel sat at a table to her right, trembling like a leaf each time the sneering prosecutor spoke. She wasn't sure which maintenance closet they'd dug this fair-haired boy out of to defend her. She *was* sure she would have been better defended if they'd let a mop argue her case. The prosecutor, a lieutenant several years older than her in a brown-and-red belted tunic, stood up behind his table and proceeded.

"Did you speak with the privateer captain of the *Calabash* on Icacos at the —" he paused to consult the sheet in his hand and twisted his lips like he'd tasted rancid rice "— Gilded Lady Tavern?"

"I didn't know who he was. He accosted me at my table while I was drinking a beer." She tried to keep a measured tone in the face of the prosecutor's revulsion.

"Yes or no, Lieutenant?"

"Yes." She pulled her voice back from the threshold of rising.

"For what purpose?"

"He approached me. I had no purpose in speaking to him except to tell him to stop speaking to me." She pursed her lips.

"What did he say to you?" The prosecutor leaned against his table, feigning patience. His condescending lilt made Virika want to pound her fist on the ledge in front of her.

"He laughed in my face, told me I was a dog and a paid traitor for the Æcerbot Empire against 'my people.'" The members of the tribunal grimaced. Even the indirect implication of prejudice was distasteful on Invicta and throughout the Empire. She understood that Invictans could — and would — pretend a thing didn't exist by not speaking about it. She'd breached that unspoken rule openly. In her peripheral vision, she saw the judge write a note.

"Did he give you this? Your Honour, the prosecution enters exhibit B-2." He handed a plastic bag to an orderly, who approached the judge's bench with it. The judge examined the bag.

"Entered," the judge said. "Orderly, show this to the accused." The orderly placed the plastic bag on the stand where Virika sat. Inside it was an iridescent pelican-struck coin exactly like the one she'd given Alba. Her heart dropped. Heat surged down her face and neck. Her counsel hadn't informed her the coin would be brought up in trial. Had they brought Alba in for questioning, too? Did they coerce her into handing over evidence? Virika shifted in her seat. Sweat slicked her palms.

"H-how did you get this?"

"Answer the question: Did the privateer give you this coin?" The prosecutor tapped his index finger on his chin.

"Not exactly." She bit her lip.

"How did it come to be in your possession?" The judge leaned forward. A few members of the tribunal paused from taking notes.

"The privateer threw it near my feet." Virika's heart pulsed in the back of her throat, making it difficult to speak. "He asked how cheaply my allegiance could be bought."

"He threw a coin worth hundreds of sovereigns at you, the emblem of the terrorist Toussard etched into it, to test your loyalty, and you kept it for no reason?" The prosecutor scowled in mock confusion.

"Yes. N-no. By then my crew, who were in the tavern, had noticed him and I having heated words. I had them forcibly remove him from the premises."

"And you kept the coin for what purpose?" *Purpose, purpose. Everything must have a purpose and intent, a final goal.* Her thoughts careened. She'd kept it, that was all.

"I'd never seen one before. He discarded it and insulted the Empire. I brought it home as a symbol that he could not sway me. I wrote about the encounter in my log."

"Yes. Your logs have been entered into evidence. I've read them. You did not mention there was iridium in the coin. You gave it to Alba Winthrope. Why?" Virika's breath caught. She hung her head. The gaze of the members of the tribunal was as sharp and heavy as the old Terran guillotines she'd learned about in school. She crumbled.

"Because it was beautiful, and I love her." Her voice quavered. She wished she could disappear into a sinkhole.

She hated that her pathetic gesture of devotion was being contorted and put on display as proof of her guilt.

"Could you speak up, Lieutenant? Some of the tribunal couldn't hear you."

Virika cleared her throat. "I gave it to Alba Winthrope because I'm in love with her. The privateer was uncouth. I did not want to repeat the scoundrel's denigration of the Empire in my logs." A ripple of disapproval passed through the officials in front of her. The eternal burn of shame flared within her — homosexuality, though not illegal, was yet another thing they did not acknowledge out loud on Invicta.

"I see. Do you love Invicta, Lieutenant? Do you love the Æcerbot Empire?" The prosecutor scratched his head.

"Yes." She squared her shoulders, regaining her composure.

"Did you take this coin as payment from the privateer to bring harm to Captain Whitehall?"

"What? No!"

"Lieutenant Lyric stated during our investigation that he'd seen the privateer hand you a coin and that you accepted it willingly."

"Lyric is a liar."

The prosecutor waved his hand in dismissal and reached over his table for another piece of evidence. "Your Honour, the prosecution would like to submit article C-1 into record." He handed another plastic bag to the orderly, who then brought it to the judge to be examined.

"Show this to the defendant."

Once again, the orderly placed the evidence on the ledge in front of Virika.

"Do you recognize the packet in the bag, Lieutenant?"

*You know I do*, she thought. *You took it from my apartment.*

"Yes. I brought it home from Icacos. A woman at a fruit stand gave it to me."

"What is it?"

"A luck charm."

"What kind of luck charm?"

"From the old Antillean religions on Terra," she said through gritted teeth. There was an audible gasp from the tribunal. She should have thrown the packet away when she had the chance. Every answer the prosecutor extracted from her made her appear more guilty and transgressive. He was tightening a literal and figurative noose about her neck.

"Are you a believer in the old religions, Lieutenant?"

"No. I believe in the Æcerbot Empire and its cherished emperor, and that we have been blessed to leave unfertile Terra behind. I have no other god."

"Why did you take the packet if you didn't believe it had value?"

"The fruit seller was an old woman. I humoured her. She reminded me of my mother."

"Is your mother a believer of the old religions?" His eyes widened.

"*No*," she blurted out, not wanting to compromise her mother's safety. "No. She loves the Empire as much as I do."

"I see. And you had no idea that the contents of the packet contained dormant bacteria that mimicked the effects of the fevers?"

She jerked her head back in surprise. "The old woman said not to drink it but not that it could make you sick."

41

"Yet the symptoms Captain Whitehall suffered before he died were the exact ones caused by ingesting such a mixture — the toxicology report we submitted into evidence proves it. And he did die painfully, Lieutenant." Again, she envisioned the captain on the floor of his hospital room gasping at her like a suffocating eel. "Did you poison Captain Whitehall's food or drink, Lieutenant?"

"I did no such thing. I had nothing to do with his illness. I loved him as dearly as I loved my own father." Her voice broke. She covered her face. The tribunal's stare weighed on her. She took her hands away.

"Murder, Lieutenant. The captain was murdered with the same bacteria you brought back to your lodgings. Is that why the privateer paid you? Is that why they let you pass unharassed through the skip gates? Do you expect us to believe these are all coincidences?" The condescending veneer in his voice dropped. His questions came at her like blows to the chest. She could barely catch her breath to answer them.

"I did —"

"No further questions, Your Honour."

"I did not kill Captain Whitehall." She gripped the ledge in front of her and looked at the judge. "I would have died for him. I would die for the Empire. I would die to protect you, Your Honour, and every member of this tribunal." She exhaled. "Lyric wanted command. Somehow, he concocted this scenario. I never meant to hurt anyone by bringing the packet or coin back. I didn't know anything about the bacteria. I don't know how he came into contact with it or swallowed it. My parents taught me to work hard and be grateful for the opportunities we gained here on Invicta.

Killing Whitehall goes against everything I've lived for and worked towards since I was a little girl." She shook, all her stoic varnish stripped away. She would have thrown herself on her knees at the judge's mercy if she could have done so.

The judge spoke, unmoved by her plea. "Defence counsel, you may redirect the witness."

Virika remained on the stand, stunned. Her stomach was lead heavy as she fixed her eyes on her ineffectual counsel. He'd done nothing to protect her or prevent the prosecution's manipulative questioning. How could he possibly salvage any of her testimony now? She began to think they'd assigned him to her specifically *not* to defend her in this sham of a trial.

He stood and licked his lips. "T-tell us in your own words about the medical attention you sought for Captain Whitehall when he fell ill." His voice faltered as he spoke. She pulled at her collar in an attempt to ease the choking sense of doom closing in on her.

The tribunal took a day to reach its verdict. Virika stood next to her counsel with her hands behind her back while they filed in from their sequestered quarters. The judge spoke once they'd taken their seats.

"On the charge of sedition, how do you find Lieutenant Virika Sameroo?" the judge asked after he'd gone through the formalities of ensuring they'd adhered to the codes of conduct in reaching their verdict.

The spokesperson for the tribunal stood. "On the charge of sedition, we find the accused guilty." She continued, but

Virika heard nothing more. She disassociated from the present, became unmoored. Pressure in her chest squeezed her lungs. Her heart shuddered in her ears. *Guilty*. Every moment, every step on the long path she'd trudged towards raising her family out of their scrape-by existence in Paria was snatched away. She clung to hope. This could not be happening. Not after all she'd given of herself to the merchant marines and Æcerbot. Surely the judge would intervene on her behalf.

"Virika Sameroo." The judge shattered her trance. "You have been found guilty on the charges of sedition, treason, conspiracy, murder, assault, and resisting arrest. Before the court sentences you to the mandatory terms for each charge, is there anything you would like us to take into consideration?" The courtroom officials' attention rounded on her like blades.

"Tell my mother I stood up for my innocence and the values she raised me with. I want her to know she did not fail." She bit her tongue to stop herself from mentioning Alba and fell silent.

"Noted." The judge coughed as he swiped through the screen in front of him. He made a few notes then addressed her. "The charges you've been found guilty of are a grave threat to the security of the Empire and to Æcerbot's way of life. A way of life into which your family was welcomed." He sipped from a glass of water on his desk. "Virika Sameroo you are forthwith sentenced in accordance with Æcerbot law to five consecutive life sentences to be completed on Tintaris. No early release shall be granted due to the severity of your crimes. Bailiffs, please remand the prisoner into custody. Members of the court tribunal, thank you for your service. Please return to your quarters for debriefing, after which you will be dismissed. This tribunal is adjourned." The judge took his mallet and hit the gong on his desk. It rang out with a finality in the courtroom that struck Virika cold. She could not bear to look at any of the witnesses to her fate as they whispered and began to exit the room.

The bailiffs' hands clamped around her shoulders and wrists. Terror exploded inside her but struggling would get her nowhere. She let them lead her from the court-room into the temporary holding cells as meek as a lamb in spring.

# FOUR
# THE PIT

Virika spent the following weeks in a holding cell at the end of a dark hall separated from other prisoners waiting to be transferred to different prison facilities. The other inmates had barked at her and rattled the bars of their cells as she was paraded past them when she'd arrived.

"Dog!" they howled.

Where once she'd commanded respect over the vast breadth of Æcerbot space, her world had now collapsed to a ten-by-ten room with only a cot and a toilet. The cell was barely enough space to contain her fury. Her incompetent counsel requested a meeting with her a few days after her conviction.

"Tell him to choke on rocks. I want new counsel. I want a retrial," was her reply.

"Ha!" The guard in a red tunic who'd delivered her counsel's message snickered. "That's not how it works here, Captain Dog."

A few years into her active service, Virika had been involved in transferring prisoners to remote prison facilities off Invicta. She'd never escorted anyone convicted of treason to Tintaris, but under her guard inmates had been allowed to request new counsel and even to communicate with their families.

As she recalled those convicts, she realized all of them had been Invictan-born. The rules she'd pledged her life to uphold did not seem to apply to her in any fashion. She'd defended everyone else's right to a fair trial and had not been entitled to one herself.

In the dark, simulated night, thoughts of her mother haunted her. Two empty seats at the table in her Paria apartment and an empty future to go along with them. What had she been told about Virika? How would she manage without the extra money that Virika sent her? The community would rally to her. Charlie, Audette down the hall, and the neighbourhood women would help her. They had to. It was the only way her mother would survive.

Deeper into the nights, she brooded over Alba and the curve of her mouth around the words *I love you, kiss me, don't leave* just two days before Virika's arrest. Lyric must have told Andilet about the coin, and the attaché must have forced Alba to hand it over. They'd never kept their affair a secret. The prosecutor had used that to bias the tribunal against her. Maybe he'd threatened Alba with charges of treason or told her he'd ruin her life. Alba's father and family were poor, too, and she was upwardly mobile. Lyric could destroy her as easily as he'd destroyed Virika.

Virika wished she could see her mother and Alba one last time. She wanted to tell them she would be all right if they would try to be all right for her, that she loved them beyond life itself. She had not received a word from either Alba or her mother since her arrest.

"Has there been a message from my mother?" she begged one morning when a guard brought her a bowl of coarse meal.

"I'm your mother, Lieutenant," the guard shouted. Virika bottled up her rage and didn't ask again. Wrath festered within her like an ulcer now that the initial shock of the trial and verdict had ebbed. The memory of Whitehall be her witness, if she set foot in Elmet again, Lyric would be brought low before her for putting her here. That spoiled rich boy would be sorry for the hurt he caused to everyone dear to her. She would wipe the smugness from his face by smashing it into the granite base floor. He knew better than anyone that she'd never betray Whitehall. Her hate for him chewed at her insides and guttered her appetite while she awaited her transfer.

"Moving day!" one of the guards mocked when the lights came on after another sleepless night. Four of them crowded into her cell, consuming the little space and air she had. They were putting their hands on her body in places she didn't want them. Having broken an officer's nose, she was never moved without at least four guards to handle her. They restrained her and pushed her out of the cell, past the row of inmates and through a narrow corridor. They came to a series of secured iron inner gates that led out of the dim temporary prison and onto a launch pad splashed in warm, concentrated orange Invictan sun. She'd barely blinked the pain of the sudden light away before she was thrust into the armoured transport craft that would take her, she assumed, to Tintaris.

"The Pit," as those in the service referred to the dwarf planet, had been mined to exhaustion and repurposed as a military prison for the criminals that Æcerbot needed to forget. It stirred an uneasiness she thought was buried in her childhood. One she could not easily define. It lived in the back of all Invictan children's minds as a reprimand for unbecoming behaviour. *You'd better behave, or you'll end up in the Pit.*

She shuddered. No officer willingly put in to serve there. Living in that hollowed-out place bore into them, hardening their hearts and scooping out their souls. There'd been stories of Pit guards on leave in Elmet or on holiday in the provinces who were shadows of the people their families had known and loved.

She'd never travelled to Tintaris with the fleet. There had never been any reason to go. It was a far-flung planet in a system shared by several of the empires. The prison itself, she had heard, was archaic, nothing more than a concrete cage beneath a ruin Æcerbot had found when they claimed the territory. The crudeness was part of the punishment — the torture of the place. The Pit was as far from the safety, progress, comfort, technology, and *light* of the Empire as one could be. No prisoner had ever been released or escaped. It was a one-way trip for the condemned.

She was forced to sit at one end of the transport and strapped to her seat. Minutes later, another set of guards appeared and shoved a young man inside. He was thin and tanned — another Antillean immigrant.

"I'm innocent." Stubborn hope persisted in his demeanour. Virika pitied him despite being in the exact situation herself.

"Shut up." One of the guards hit the back of the man's knees with his club. The man yelped and crumpled onto a seat. "Everyone's innocent in the Pit. Isn't that right, Captain?" The guard glared at Virika, his words twisting out of his mouth like a venomous root.

Virika stayed silent and avoided eye contact with her fellow inmate as he was pulled upright and buckled in tight. He was purposefully searching her out, eyes darting, wanting to connect with her gaze for a moment of shared experience and camaraderie. He reminded her of an injured bird she'd found as a child on Orinoco. The little blue and grey tanager had been caught between a cat's paws. Its wings were broken and bent back on themselves. She'd shooed the cat away and brought the woeful creature to her mother.

"Fix it, Ma," she'd told her. Her mother took the bird in her hands.

"Some things you can't fix, Viri," her mother said. Her eyes shone with tears as they watched the poor bird die.

Virika could not give her fellow inmate any reassurance. It would have been a betrayal. It would have given him hope when there was none. She kept her attention focused on the wall in front of her. Avoiding each other would lessen the likelihood of them being beaten.

No warning before takeoff. From her own experience and from the turbulence they experienced on ascent, Virika knew when they'd quit the atmosphere. Her fellow prisoner, who she now thought of as Tanager, threw up on himself. The guards, disgusted, towelled him off so the cabin wouldn't reek.

The long, monotonous ride combined with her sapped adrenaline after being moved left Virika exhausted. She drifted off on a wave of sleep. Before slipping from consciousness, she heard her mother's voice: *Viri.*

The jolt at entry and exit through the skip gate shook her awake. Tanager threw up again. His face scrunched with nausea.

There were no portholes on the ship, no view of the approach to Tintaris. No perspective, nothing to attach her fate or future to other than the grey transport wall in front of her face and the sour stench of bile.

The guards unbuckled them both, when the transport landed. The hold's door opened and steps appeared. Weak violet light filtered into the cabin. The guards shoved Tanager and Virika out. Waiting at the bottom of the steps were four additional guards seated on three-wheeled vechs. Their faces were hidden by blank copper-coloured masks. The eyes, covered in black mesh, resembled an insect's compound eyes. The image of a horde of locusts came to her, unblinking, unfeeling, and inhuman.

The dirt beneath their feet was sandy and grey. In the distance loomed a slate-coloured stone fortress that housed a severe upright keep, singular and desolate against the backdrop of the contusion-purple sky. Virika's heart dropped at its bleakness.

She and Tanager were bound around their waists

approximately a metre apart from each other with heavy steel chains. Their hands were cuffed in front of them. The lead of their chain was hooked to a hitch on the back of one of the two three-wheeled vechs ahead of them. The two other guards positioned their vechs behind them. All revved their engines, filling the air with stomach-churning exhaust. Virika ducked her head and breathed as shallowly as she could. Tanager inhaled and coughed, his lungs full of chemicals.

"Out!" one of the guards called. The convoy yanked them forward by their lead. Virika followed at a jog while Tanager tumbled and fell behind her, jerking her backward. This prompted the guards ahead of them to accelerate, dragging him and forcing Virika to run while being pulled backward by his weight and inhaling exhaust from the vechs. When the guards tired of their tortuous game of tug of war, they slowed to a crawl. Virika tried to speak but only managed a whisper from her burning throat.

"Stand up. It's not much farther," she said to Tanager.

"I didn't do anything." His voice was as raw and jagged as glass.

Virika exhaled. "I believe you," she said. She started walking again without looking back.

The trek stretched for hours in the brick oven heat. When they arrived, the looming iron gates screeched open against the dry desert air. They were led into a wide, square pea gravel courtyard. Watchtowers were placed at regular intervals along the outer wall. Virika had learned as a child that their Terran predecessors had built castles long ago as a means of keeping enemy armies out. Here, the walls, towers, and gates were meant to keep her, an enemy of the Empire, inside. A chill skittered through her as she considered the barbaric place she was about to enter. Her existence would be swallowed by darkness and time. The tower guards remained unseen above and yet their gazes burdened her like an invisible boot pressed on her neck.

The locust guards on the three-wheelers parked a few metres from the iron doors of the keep and unhooked the lead from the metal hitch. The rear guards came up close behind Virika and Tanager; their breathing was dry and light against their masks. The back of Virika's throat was raw and tasted of blood from inhaling sand. Each gulp of air was like swallowing a scrap of sandpaper.

"Move." The guards drove Virika and Tanager forward, clubs jabbed into the smalls of their backs, forcing them into the keep.

She couldn't see at first. It was darker under the fluorescent lights in the keep than in the feeble violet daylight outside. The air was damp like a wet animal tongue. She shivered. In front of them were desks arranged in a rectangle with a thick transparent barrier around them. Inside sat several guards wearing the inscrutable locust facemasks. Four of them left through the central desk door at the back of the transparent enclosure and came around to the front. They separated Virika and Tanager. The convoy guards then took them both to opposite ends of the square room where there were doors inset into the walls.

"Strip," one of the intake guards ordered Virika. Her chest and face grew hot as she undressed in front of them. Defiant, she stared straight into their soulless eyes. *Let them look*, she thought. *Pigs.*

"I've seen better bitches," a locust guard quipped as if reading her mind. Once she was naked and they'd taken their time raking their gazes over her, a coarse pair of pants, a short-sleeved shirt, and rubber shoes were thrown at her. She slipped them on and stood still.

"Hold out your wrist," another guard commanded. Virika did as ordered. Being manhandled was a part of her inescapable hellish existence. While one guard grabbed her shoulders, another gripped her upper arm and elbow.

Tanager shrieked from the other side of the keep. Virika ground her teeth, shutting out his misery and the knowledge that she would soon experience the very same pain. A third guard positioned a branding wand two inches above her skin. She recoiled, tried to yank her arm away, but they held her fast. The guard with the wand pulled its trigger. The scent of her own singed flesh turned her stomach. Her mind blanked, cleared by searing, white hot pain.

They let go. Cauterized into her inner wrist was a circle with an X crossed over it. The mark of a traitor. Her focus wavered. She could barely understand their instructions over the burning sting blocking out all her other senses. She shook, straining to keep herself from screaming in anguish.

"Cry, Captain. You have no dignity to lose here," one of the locusts hissed. The guard behind her grabbed the base of her head with both hands, thumbs digging into the soft space where her neck ended and her skull began, and gripped either side of her chin tightly with his fingers. The locust with the wand now held a razor. He began to shave off her thick black hair. Her mother had sobbed the day Virika shaved it for entrance into the academy; she'd been overjoyed when Virika had been permitted to let it grow out after being commissioned. It fell to the floor in clumps now.

"Don't move," the locust with the razor laughed in her ear. "I wouldn't want to cut you by mistake." Virika's arm was on fire. She couldn't process what was happening.

A door opened on the other side of the keep. She watched as Tanager was pushed through by two other guards. She knew she'd never see him again. *I know you're innocent,* was all she could think as the door clicked shut behind him. *I believe you, fragile Tanager.*

When the Locust was finished shaving Virika's head, another placed their palm on a security lock. A metal door near her slid into the wall. Two guards shoved her through the threshold onto a shadowy landing. The door slid closed behind them. The air was mouldy and damp. Stairs descended a few metres away, curving into a spiral. Scrape marks textured the walls. *Who had carved this all out so long ago?* she wondered.

"Move." One of the guards pushed her again. She gripped the rail, ignoring the pain in her arm, and began the long descent.

After each flight, they came to another landing with a metal door inserted into the stone walls. Adjacent to each door was a security pad. Each time she hoped they'd reached the right floor, they pushed her towards the next flight. Virika counted eight doors. When they'd arrived at the bottom of the stairwell, nine flights down, a guard touched their hand to the pad on the wall again. The door slid into the wall, revealing a short hallway. The air was heavier and thicker, like it had not been stirred in ages. The guards kicked her forward.

"In," one said. This hallway was even gloomier than the stairwell had been. The quiet was so all-encompassing it was disorienting. There was one door inset in each wall. Was there someone else locked away down here with her? The guards opened the door on the right and thrust her inside. The door clicked shut behind her without ceremony — her life cut off in silence. Their footsteps retreated.

She was alone.

"Hello?" she yelled. No one responded, not even her own echo. Could her voice carry outside of the cell? She'd heard the guards' footsteps as they left. Perhaps the walls and doors were so thick they were soundproof? More likely it was that she was alone in this part of the Pit. No one she loved knew where she was. She'd never hear from or see her mother or Alba again.

She scanned the room: a mattress on a cot, a toilet, and four cold stone walls. Similar accommodations to her holding cell on Invicta. There wasn't even a sheet to wrap around her neck to end her life. Another surge of exhaustion and dizziness hit her. The brand on her wrist pulsed with pain. She lay down on the mattress and let unconsciousness submerge her for the second time that day, wishing it was death itself come to kiss her goodnight.

She woke parched. How long had she been asleep? Did it matter? Days and time only had meaning when they were filled with activity and purpose. What was her purpose now that she was locked in a box by herself?

There was no hope for an appeal or some miraculous declaration of a mistrial. Whitehall was dead. She didn't want Alba to risk her own position on her behalf. Her mother couldn't navigate Æcerbot legal bureaucracy. Even if she could, where would the money for legal fees come from now that Virika wasn't there to supplement her mother's income? Who knew if the justice department would even entertain an appeal. Virika stood and paced the width of the tiny room, the burn stinging to the point of tears every time she moved her forearm.

How do you live when the centre of the universe, the Empire you have forsaken your sense of self for, greedily accepts your blood sacrifice then casts you from its sight the second it is displeased? She knew nothing of the old religions of her forbearers. They'd been stripped from her and her family.

The memory of a prayer ceremony she'd witnessed as a little girl on Orinoco whispered to her. The scent of sandalwood and smoke had encircled her as she sat next to her father, swept up in a rhythmic chant. The resonant blow of a conch shell vibrated the air. Aromas and sounds filled her mind but were connected to nothing, rendering the sensations meaningless. She had no faith to sustain her.

"For the Empire!" she screamed. She'd taken on extra duties, worked four times as hard as everyone around her to rise through the ranks, and when she'd successfully brought their precious iridium to port, the Empire had discarded her on the whim of a boy she wouldn't fuck. A man-child who wanted power he couldn't wield. It had all been for naught. Now both she and her mother were as good as dead. A desolate sob broke from her lips. The locust guard had been right. She didn't have to hold back. There was no one here to care.

A panel at the bottom of the cell door slid open and a tray was shoved through. The panel slid closed. Virika eyed the food on it. Hard bread, a piece of grey matter that she guessed was supposed to be cheese. She wanted her mother's cooking. The flavour of ginger, garlic, black pepper, and culantro engulfed her tongue. There was care and time put into everything her mother made. Ma planned meals a week ahead of time so she could marinate meats and fish for days before stewing or currying them. Virika's mouth watered. Food had been the only part of her heritage that she'd been allowed to keep openly. She'd even tried to cook Antillean food for herself in her on-base apartment. She smiled, remembering the hard, square-shaped roti she'd made for Alba.

"This is what it's supposed to taste like," she explained when she brought Alba to dinner to meet her mother in Paria.

"It's better than yours," Alba joked. Virika agreed. She'd always revelled in the food that had nourished her ancestors, from the Caribbean on Terra to Exterran space.

That had been part of her crime, hadn't it? How had she ever thought she was one of them, that she'd assimilated, when she was never fully Invictan? It showed on her skin, affected her taste buds, and made her pity a fruit stall woman who reminded her of her poor brown mother.

She bit into the cheese. Lyric's self-satisfied smirk wriggled to the surface of her mind. Her gorge rose. She started to spit the cheese out, paused, and forced herself to swallow it. Æcerbot wanted her gone, but they'd been too cowardly to sentence her to death and didn't want to stoke unrest among the working poor of Paria. So, they'd dumped her here to die in the dark. She wouldn't give them the satisfaction of aiding in her demise.

Spite. That's what she'd live for.

She finished eating the bread and cheese and shoved the empty metal plate up to the door.

# FIVE

# ETCHED

Virika examined her prison. The lights turned on and off for an equal number of hours, she approximated. This allowed her to keep a rough count of the days that passed. She got down on her hands and knees during her lighted hours and scoured the cell's corners. There was no trace of anyone who might have been held in it before her. The mattress was made of thick canvas stuffed with straw or some other natural material on top of a basic metal bed frame. It didn't hold its shape and was uncomfortable to sleep on. She pulled at the covering. There was no way she could rip it apart to use the fabric for anything.

She was given a bucket of water to wash herself with once a week. Within two months her cycle had stopped. Had they forced amenorrhea on her? They had control over her body — of course they'd take that from her without her consent. It made her skin crawl.

She'd lost her appetite during the trial and the early days of her imprisonment. Her ribs had grown visible mimicking a cage themselves. Her jawline grew sharp. She could make out the phantom of her reflection in her wash bucket. Who was the gaunt creature she'd become? With her fractalizing spite came a piercing hunger she had to sate.

Eight different types of meals: bland porridges, boiled vegetables, rubber meat, hard breads, rice, beans, thin soups, a lemon to keep scurvy away — and not a drop of salt or spice. Not inedible and enough to keep her alive, but not enjoyable for human consumption either.

The dark hours were a yawning abyss. She could not sleep. Her thoughts spiraled between worrying about her mother, dread at the thought of Alba loving someone else, and bitter hate for every Empire official who chose not to speak on her behalf. When she managed to rest, her dreams were filled with scenes of her youth in Paria. She saw herself kissing Daria, her first love, or setting off fireworks with her friends at night for Invicta day. She soothed the grief of waking to find that those days were dead by filling her lighted hours with push-ups and squats and daydreams of the future she might have lived.

By her count, once every fifteen days she was taken up the winding stairs by the guards, who she came to regard as living locusts, and allowed to walk the circular gravel court-yard twice while under watch. Guns trained on her from every tower.

The violet sun hurt her eyes and the wind chafed her skin, but she relished it. Even the clouds in the purple sky were a joyous break from the monotony of her dank cell. Panic bubbled in her each time the locusts shoved her back in the desolate Pit, with its unyielding walls.

After six months, she estimated, they entered her cell and shaved off her matted hair.

On what she guessed was the anniversary of her imprisonment, she was brushed aside as the locusts, along
with a prison inspector, surveyed her cell.

"Are you being fed?" the inspector asked without ceremony. Hers was the only unmasked face Virika had seen
since she'd been thrown in the Pit. Transfixed, she stared
at the inspector's green eyes, and studied her small mouth.
Seeing another human face after being locked away so long
was engrossing. The inspector twisted her lips at Virika's
gawking. She stepped back before she continued. "Do they
let you wash? Do you get the opportunity to exercise?"

Virika recalled the prosecutor berating her with questions. The inspector wanted a specific answer. Complaining
might result in punishment.

"Yes." Would her situation change if she said no? The
inspection was a farce just as her trial had been.

The inspector grunted in response and walked out the
door with the locusts fast behind her. The visit was over as
abruptly as it had started.

One morning, during her mandatory walk in the gravel
yard around the keep, Virika noticed a darker-coloured
stone among the others. On her second circuit, she bent
over and picked it up, pretending to adjust her shoe while
she slipped the rock inside it. The movement took all of a
second or two before she straightened to stand.

Locked back in her cell, she pulled the stone out of
her shoe and examined it. It was larger than the pea gravel
in the courtyard and had a bit of weight to it. She could

hold it between her thumb and index finger comfortably. A long-stifled impulse from before her academy days bloomed inside her when she'd noticed it. Her father had bought her a sketchbook and a set of pencils with part of his first payment from the building docks. Drawing had been her solace at that age. She'd plastered her tiny bedroom walls with sketches of the immigrant ship and the little stone house they'd left behind on Orinoco. *Daddy always knew what I needed,* she thought as she assessed the space below her prison cot.

She pulled the frame into the middle of the room. Her anger had remained molten, but her memory of Lyric's pompous face had blurred. Hunched over on her knees, she used the point of the rock to scratch the outline of Lyric's head into the floor, back and forth, back and forth, until it was etched in the stone and her hand had cramped.

It had been so long since she'd gripped a piece of charcoal, chalk, or any artistic tool. She focused on the image in her head and lost herself in the movement, muscle memory overtaking her. She added to it each day, filling in the arrogant shine in Lyric's expression, his thin lips and blocky chin. She outlined his neck and body. The stone wore down gradually. She had to wait for another outing in the courtyard to find a suitable replacement. She couldn't find one the next time she was allowed up and had to wait another fifteen days. While she waited, she set to work making pigments to wash over her drawing from the water she used for bathing and the scraps of vegetables she'd saved from her meals. She couldn't achieve the vibrancy of colour she wanted. How she longed to visit the art supply in Elmet, near the art college. She would spend her entire life comparing subtle shades of red if she were given the chance. All she could manage here were shades of tangerine and very a sandy tan. She was proud of herself for creating the dyes with zero resources. She etched her mother, with her long hair and worried brow, and then finally Alba's large, clear eyes and beautiful mouth, using more smuggled rocks. The thought of them all, even hateful Lyric underneath her cot, made her sleep more restful and her days less lonely.

She was mixing a wash with scraps of carrot when the hall door opened and footsteps approached her cell. She poured the mixture in the toilet and flushed before two locusts entered, followed by the inspector.

Had another year passed? She'd lost count of the days. She stood with her back pressed against the wall. The locusts crowded inside. The anomaly of seeing the inspector's face astonished her again: the movement of the woman's facial muscles, the flex of her neck — it was surreal. The inspector rattled off her usual questions while the locusts examined every corner of the room and the mattress. They pulled the bed frame away from the wall. Virika tensed.

"Inspector, you need to see this," one of the locusts said. Virika's mouth went dry.

"Get in the corner. Hands on the wall where I can see them," the other locust ordered.

The inspector stepped deeper into the room. "Hmmm," she said. "Perhaps you should have focused your energy on art instead of treason. Put her in the other cell. Have this ground down and sanded over. Then put her back."

Something cracked inside Virika. A broken whimper escaped her lips. *No*, she mouthed to the wall. She fought every instinct to elbow the locust standing behind her in the chest.

"Did you say something?" he spat. She kept silent, too distraught to protest. They pushed her out of the room and shoved her into the cell across the hall. She fell on the cot, choking on her sobs. An abyss rent the insides of her chest. She'd poured everything she had left into that etching. It had kept her alive. The spite and anger and small amount of joy that had sustained her drained away, replaced by a creeping numbness. *Why couldn't they let me keep it?* Voiceless spasms racked her body until being awake was too much for her to bear. She emptied her mind, mirroring the state of her heart, and forced herself to sleep.

When she woke, the lights were still on. Would they move her back? Her stomach growled. When was the last time she'd eaten? She stared at the wall across from her and noticed something scratched into the corner near the door. She slipped off the cot and crouched to read it.

*Death is better*, it said.

Two locusts entered the cell, one carrying a long cane.

"Hands and feet apart against the wall," ordered the one carrying the stick.

The swish of the lash sliced the air. There was a thwack

before the bite of the cane cut into her flesh. She fought back a wail, flinching as the pain sunk into her. It radiated across her back.

"Straighten up, Captain. At attention or it'll be double," the locust hissed. Virika braced herself. They whipped her twice more. Her skin burned as welts erupted in the wake of the switch. The locust with the cane stepped away and opened the cell door. The other held the door open while the first crossed the hall and opened Virika's cell door. Virika turned around, arching her back against the deepening ache. The locust in the room stared at her until the first guard called for them to cross the hall back into her cell.

"Inside," said the one who'd whipped her. Virika entered her cell and the door slid behind her. Her clothes stuck to her welts. She pulled her shirt off carefully, let it fall to the floor and shuffled over to the cot frame. She checked the slab underneath it. Her drawings had been sanded away and smoothed over. Erased, like she had been. Like her entire life had never existed.

The panel at the bottom of the door slid open and a metal tray was shoved through. On it was a bowl of thin pheasant soup and some hard bread. There was a tube of cream next to the plate.

"Ha," she laughed mirthlessly. "Yes. Starve and beat me, but an infection! We can't have that." She eyed the wooden spoon next to the soup. She took it over to the cot and broke the scoop off against its frame. The remaining handle was splintered and sharp. She sat in the middle of the cell, held her right hand out in front of her, aimed the ragged point at the X within the scarred-over brand they'd burned into her, and plunged it into the vein in her wrist over and over. She ignored the pain, ignored her entire body screaming for her to stop each time she pulled her arm back and thrust the piece of wood down to gouge herself. She dropped the handle when a steady seep of blood oozed from her wrist. She lay on her side then and waited for unconsciousness.

At some point — she could not tell how much time had passed — someone entered her cell.

"Let me die," she begged.

"No." The voice was warm, like a soft breeze.

Virika woke in her cot with bandages around her wrist and wearing a new shirt. Why was she awake? She didn't want to be alive. She lay there staring at the wall until the shuffle of feet sounded outside her cell door. The panel slid open. Her meal was placed inside as usual. She dragged herself from the cot and crawled over to the panel.

"Why won't you let me die?" No sob broke her voice this time. The question was flat and matter of fact. The panel slid closed. There was a hesitation in the footsteps outside the door before the locust walked away. Virika stared at the food in front of her. No utensils. Sliced boiled meat to eat with her hands, some bread, and a quarter of an . . . apple? She seized the fruit and bit into it. Her mouth watered. Her tongue contorted around its sweet-ness. When she was finished, she put the plate up against the panel and waited for the locust to retrieve it.

The panel slid open and two hands reached inside to collect the tray. Virika moved closer to peer through the opening.

"Thank you for the apple," she said.

"You're welcome," the locust whispered, shutting the door quickly as if Virika were a contagion.

Over time, Virika's wrist healed, and fruit she hadn't eaten since childhood continued to appear on her dinner tray. There were Antillean chenets and governor's plums that were as sweet as syrup. Once, a slice of overripe Tollian mango seasoned with garlic and pepper, reminiscent of a chow she'd had at an Orinoco street festival as a girl, supplemented her otherwise flavourless food.

"Did you like it?" the locust asked after every meal. Virika found herself on the brink of tears each time.

"Yes," she answered. How finite her being had become. Her entire existence centred on an arbitrary piece of fruit. But it was more than the sweetness on her tongue. It was the inquiry as to whether she liked it — that it mattered to someone that she enjoyed it. That was what undid her.

"Why did you save me?" she asked one evening after finishing a piece of pineapple. She sat on the ground near the opening in the door. The locust stood on the other side. They'd never spoken at length before. This evening, Virika sensed a change through the thick metal door.

"We do have hearts behind our masks, some of us."

The locust's voice was smooth and dulcet. It was the voice she'd heard before she lost consciousness after trying to kill herself.

"Then why work here?" Despite the locust's kindness, Virika was wary. What if this was a trap that would get her punished? The locust sat down near the open panel.

"Why did you join the merchant marine? You of all people, a descendant of Terran indentured servants and enslaved people? Did you think you could change the system internally? Did you think you could make them treat you as an equal if you behaved perfectly? You were wrong about that weren't you? I've been wrong, too." Regret tinged the locust's resonant voice.

"You know all about me," Virika said. "I know nothing about you." The locust shifted in place, wrestling with the statement.

"What would you like to know?" Their words slowed as if they were aware they were skirting a risk.

"Tell me your earliest memory of feeling alone."

The locust shifted again. They were silent for a long while. Virika thought they'd get up and leave without answering the question.

"I grew up on Vantalus, Tintaris's sister planet. Once, when I was five, the children in the suburb where we lived organized a war game." Their voice had taken on a dreamy, unfocused quality. "None of them wanted me on their side. Neither group. I was too small, a girl, and slow. I sat alone in front of my house and watched them pretend to ambush and shoot each other with lasers. I wanted to join, but they didn't want me. I couldn't make myself go inside. I stayed and watched and let their exclusion hurt me."

"Does that still fester after all this time? The feeling of wanting to belong to a side but being prevented from joining because of who you are?" Virika could not subdue the sneer that settled on her face. It coloured her voice. "Have you found your place, your side, here in the Pit?"

"No. I don't belong here. No one belongs in the Pit." The locust picked up Virika's tray and closed the sliding door. Shortly afterwards the lights clicked off. Virika was left in the dark with the echoes of her childhood spent playing war games in Paria's streets, where her side always won.

The locust, who asked to be called Kalima, dawdled outside Virika's cell door in the evenings. There were no other prisoners this deep in the Pit, and Kalima's main duties during her shift involved setting out and removing dinner trays and patrolling the upper halls when she felt like it. With everyone under biolock and key so far underground, indoor guards were left to their own devices during the night hours. No one questioned or reported what any of them did with their time throughout the long stretches of darkness.

The desire for interaction gnawed at Virika. She welcomed the chance to talk, to hear a voice other than her own, even if it was the voice of one of her captors from behind a cell door. Kalima spoke as if they were friends meeting in an Elmet square over a shot of Bently's, for old time's sake. She told Virika of her small house not far from the Pit, filled with sketches and paint and of the desert garden she tended in her backyard.

"It upset me when they destroyed your etchings," she said. "Part of me would die if someone took my sketches from me. Who were the people you drew?"

Virika's story tumbled out of her like a rock fall. Kalima listened the whole way through, never interrupting her once.

"I'm sorry," Kalima said. "I believe you are innocent. You had no reason to kill Whitehall or commit treason with your career on the fast track."

This rendered Virika speechless. Tears, heavy and hot, streamed down her face. She never thought she'd hear those words out of anyone's mouth, let alone the mouth of a locust.

"Tell me how you ended up here," Virika asked when she could speak again. "No one chooses the Pit willingly."

Kalima said she had come to work at the prison when the government she'd served under as a bureaucrat in Vantalus's capital fell under charges of corruption.

"I did nothing wrong." She banged the door between them as she spoke, making Virika jump. "Afterwards, no one would hire me. The embarrassment and the doubts about my character were too much for my partner to handle at her job. My life fell apart. The Pit was as good as any place to disappear and build a quiet life. No one asks you about your past here." Virika heard her sigh. "Except you."

"My life was never quiet until I was imprisoned," Virika said. "We were poor, but Paria was filled with laughter and music and food. I played cricket with the neighbourhood kids. Art school was full of exhibitions and friends. At the academy, it was bells and drills and fellow marines and travel. I miss people. I miss my mother. I miss Alba."

Kalima was silent, as she always was when she was thinking.

"I'll let you sit in the hall with me, if it would help you feel less alone," she said.

Virika went rigid. "You'd let me out? Why?" She laughed at the thought of policing herself in prison, of questioning being let out when she'd been labelled a threat to the safety of the Empire and locked up unjustly. Who knew what was waiting for her in the corridor if she said yes.

"There's no way to escape," Kalima said. "You know that yourself. If you run up the nine flights of steps *after* somehow overpowering me and somehow getting the bio-locked door open, there are eight guards waiting in the admin station armed with lasers and guns. If you get past them and into the courtyard, there are watchtower snipers surrounding the keep. And if you get past *them*, the desert will kill you." Kalima's voice held no emotion. "Besides, if I don't show up on time at the end of my shift, they'll send down a team to deal with you. It would be suicide to injure me." Virika digested Kalima's arguments. They rang with truth. A short while ago, the threat of death would have been a welcome option.

"I'd like to sit in the hall with you, Kalima," she said at last.

The door slid open and Virika stepped out. "Hello." She held her hands up in the air.

"Hi," Kalima said behind her locust mask. She spread her arms wide, as if welcoming an honoured guest to her home. "You're all right. Put your hands down."

"You keep the mask on even though I never see you behind the door?"

"I slipped it on before I let you out. I keep it with me always. It's protocol, in case I have to enter your cell." Virika blinked at the answer. "Eye contact breeds empathy." Kalima shrugged.

"Forbid us all from having empathy." Virika let the snide remark slip from her mouth before she could stop herself.

She tensed for Kalima's reaction. The locust chuckled and invited her to sit next to her on the floor of the corridor.

"Did they sterilize me by putting something in my food?" Virika demanded when they'd grown comfortable speaking to each other.

"Sterilize, permanently? No. They've stopped your ability to get pregnant by putting medication in your food. It's in case there should be any . . . contact between you and a guard. The Pit isn't a place for an infant." Kalima still wore the locust mask with its dead eyes. Virika fought against the acid clawing up her throat. She'd been right. She hadn't been given the dignity of knowing what they'd done to her body.

"In case there should be contact? As if I'd have a choice? As if contact would not be forced on me by someone? How I've escaped such horror, I don't know." She glanced up at the ceiling and shook her head.

Kalima put a hand on Virika's, and Virika knew from the pressure that Kalima had done something to keep the other locusts away. She did not dare ask what. That it had worked was enough. She pulled her hand from underneath Kalima's, bristling.

This was not friendship or, god forbid, something more. Friendship did not exist when one party kept the other under lock and key and controlled what they ate. Kalima had, whether Virika wanted her to or not, become her universe. She kept her alive, and Virika had become intimately bound to her seemingly benevolent jailor.

"What do you want from me?" Virika asked one evening after she'd eaten a sour piece of plum that made her lips pucker. Kalima ducked her head. Virika laughed, hollow and empty at the gesture. "What could you be embarrassed to tell me? I am as far from a judge as anyone could be in all of Exterran space."

"I have no one," Kalima said. "I want my life to mean something, even if it's to one person. I don't want the sole record of my days to be that of a disgraced civil-servant-cum-Pit-guard. That is all I'll ever be if I don't act." She paused. Virika sensed there was more Kalima wanted to say. Kalima cleared her throat. She put her hands to her head and slowly lifted the locust mask from her face.

Virika gasped. It had been years since she'd seen anyone's face except for the inspector who'd had her beaten and destroyed her etchings. She studied Kalima's features. She was older than Virika had anticipated. Age had carved faint crow's feet near her temples and frosted her cropped hair silver. Her brown eyes and the undertone of her skin captivated Virika.

"Y-you're Antillean?" Her breath hitched.

"On my mother's side." Kalima quirked her lips. "The Æcerbots don't read me as Antillean." She held the mask in front of her chest. "I'm going to help you escape the Pit, Captain Virika Sameroo." Virika jerked back as if she'd been smacked. She'd accepted that she'd die in the Pit. The thought of escape was as plausible as her being proclaimed emperor of the Kaspan.

"You said yourself, it would be a death wish for me to try to walk out of here alive. Even if I did escape, where would I go? Who would harbour me? I'd be an open target in the desert." Virika scowled. "How can I trust you?" She clenched her jaw, growing angry at the inherent cruelty of Kalima's suggestion.

Kalima's eyes remained fixed on Virika. Virika had grown so unaccustomed to the intensity of an open gaze that she flinched from it as if she'd touched a hot coal.

"I have a plan." Kalima slipped the mask back over her face. A jitter ran up Virika's spine as the once-more inhuman locust surveyed her. "I suppose trust doesn't exist in a place like the Pit, but this is all we both have. Have a good night, Virika," she said. "We have much to discuss."

# SIX

# KALIMA

Kalima brought a piece of charcoal with her the next evening. Virika yearned to snatch it away from her. How lovely it would feel between her fingers. How freeing it would be to trace even a simple shape onto her cell wall. Instead, she sat next to the locust mask on the cot while Kalima drew a map on the wall in front of her.

"This is the Exterran Antilles." Virika squinted, angling her head to one side.

"Yes." Kalima nodded. "Here are the three stars." She pointed with the chalk to a group of circles. "These are the planets Orinoco, Chantimelle, and Tollian." She circled a dwarf planet on the edge of the system. "Bequia is here."

"Right. What does this tiny planet light years away have to do with me escaping the Pit?" Virika crossed her arms.

"You aren't the first Antillean to be imprisoned here. Richard Toussard was locked in the cell across the hall before you." Kalima enunciated each syllable. Virika put her hand to her mouth. The faded tingle of searing cane lashes prickled across her back. The words "Death is better" scratched into the wall of the cell across from hers formed on the inside of her eyelids as she closed them.

Richard Toussard, a criminal insurgent to the Empire and a revolutionary hero to some Exterran Antilleans. It was his emblem on the privateer coin that had helped lock Virika away. He'd incited the most viable Antillean rebellion ever attempted, on tiny Bequia, almost two decades earlier. His rebels gained control of the planet and were recruiting fighters from the neighbouring Exterran Antilles for their cause when an Æcerbot force brutally beat down their faction. Bequia's streets were stained with the blood of the "terrorists" as an example to any future "savage" threats to the Empire's industry. Virika had analyzed Toussard's methods at the academy, studied how he'd secured loyalty in his followers and how Æcerbot had destroyed his cause.

"They said he was shot in a skirmish with Æcerbot forces."

"No. He was taken, with both his legs broken but alive, and brought in for interrogation." Kalima exhaled. "He refused to speak. They imprisoned him here in the weeks before they secretly executed him. He kept his resolve but had been crushed in many ways, a shadow of the presence he'd once been. Nothing like the pictures we saw of him on screens, with his fist raised in solidarity. But there was still a spark within him. Days before he was killed he told me where he and his crew had hoarded the iridium they'd siphoned from the mines in the months leading up to the revolt."

Virika stood up and pointed at the map. "Here? This nowhere dwarf planet is where they hid it? Why would he tell you this?"

"The planet has a name: Bocas. He said: 'I have no heirs. You are one of our people. You must remember what I've told you and use it when the time comes.' He spoke of the Haitian revolution long ago on Terra, and of the legacy of a man named Toussaint. I didn't know what he meant then. What time would come for a lonely woman keeping watch at the bottom of a hole? He was a remarkable person, Virika. Brave in the face of certain death. I kept his secret. I should have done more for him. His murder, *that* legacy haunts me." She paused, bitterness colouring her expression. "The Empire holds no glory for me. It spit me out like a rotten mango the moment it lost its taste for me. He knew. Toussard knew someone like you would arrive." She became animated with piercing determinism. "It won't be easy. You are going to escape the Pit, retrieve that iridium, and re-spark the rebellion that Toussard began."

Virika scoffed at the proposition. She froze when Kalima did not laugh or retract her plan.

"I've never had anything easy," Virika said, humouring this absurdity. "They disposed of me like garbage, too. Lyric was the mechanism. The Empire cannot tolerate me. I am a threat to their doctrine, to the belief that they are superior and civilized."

Virika looked back at the map. "Why did none of the empires claim this planet?"

A frown darkened Kalima's face. "Toussard said something was alive on Bocas. A force that hurt him and each of his crew in a personal way. He hid the iridium there because . . . the empires know a shadow haunts Bocas. It's cursed."

Virika rubbed her arms. There was nothing to say in response to what amounted to gibberish from a lonely woman. Kalima wiped away the star chart and took the charcoal with her before she left that evening.

"You must remember everything, Virika. We can't keep any records," she said before closing the door behind her.

Virika committed the star chart to memory so accurately she could reproduce it on her cell wall when Kalima gave her a piece of charcoal. Memorizing the passcodes and directions she needed to escape proved harder, but in time they became as sacred to her as the names of her mother and father. There was so much to remember. For months she ate, breathed, and slept Kalima's fantasy of escape, with doubt all the while panting at the back of her mind. Kalima had never detailed how she planned to get them out of the Pit — she had only explained the security systems and the layout of the keep.

Virika's dreams were clouded with stars, sand, and the spectre of death. In them, she chased Kalima through a maze in the desert, never able to catch her. At the end of the corridors she'd come upon an uncrossable chasm with a mouth that grew as its edges crumbled beneath her feet. On the other side of the void her mother and Alba begged her to leap over to them.

"I can't," she'd scream as the lip of the chasm disintegrated and she slipped into the open mouth of an enormous locust. She'd jerk awake right as its jaws closed around her, the word "out" on her tongue.

Kalima had never set a date for the execution of her plan. As time wore on, she paced more and more while quizzing Virika relentlessly on everything she'd taught her. She bit her lips until they bled when Virika couldn't remember a code or a direction correctly.

"NO!" She grabbed Virika by the arms and shook her. "Error means death, Virika," she said through gritted teeth.

Virika endured Kalima's violence, ignoring the finger-shaped bruises that purpled her forearms. There was no one Virika could complain to and no way of knowing if this was an elaborate story to trick her into getting shot. She had no reason to live. She would die here like Toussard regardless. Her mind was as captive to Kalima's whims as her physical body.

Kalima opened the cell door one day and stepped inside without a word of greeting. She produced a fluorescent blue vial and a small hacksaw from a canvas bag. She handed the saw to Virika.

"What's this for?" Virika grimaced, holding the tool away from her.

"I've never explained how you're going to escape the Pit itself. I've given you every direction and passcode but never described how you'll crawl out of this hell." Kalima uncorked the vial and drank its contents. Her lips crimped like a child tasting acrid velo juice for the first time. Virika inhaled, understanding dawning in her. Kalima slipped the vial into her pocket. "This is poison made from deadly Vanum flowers," she continued. "It will work shortly. You must listen carefully. I don't have much time to answer many quest—"

"NO!" Virika screeched. "No! You can't. This isn't for me!" She flung the hacksaw away. It clanged on the floor. She grabbed Kalima by the shoulders and shook her, forgetting Kalima's authority over her.

"I have done it, Virika. I've considered every angle, right down to your weight and height for months, years now. What do I have left to enjoy in my life? Listen to me." She gulped heavily, suppressing a gag. "You need my palm print to open the biosecurity locks." She glanced at the saw. "Wrap my hand in pieces of canvas bag, so there's no trail of blood. Carrying soiled linens out isn't something the guards upstairs would think twice about. They saw me bring the bag into the keep. The rest, you know." She swayed, breaking away from Virika as she stumbled over to sit on the bed. Voiceless rage filled Virika's throat and spilled over. Stinging tears streamed down her face.

"How dare you put me in this position." Virika could barely hold on to coherence. "My entire life I've had to be what everyone else has wanted me to be. And now, even at the bottom of a hole on a godforsaken planet, I have become the bearer of the legacy you think you want. The locusts will find me and say I've murdered you. How could you plan this without telling me? If you wanted to die, why involve me? You didn't let me die when I wanted to." She covered her face with her hands.

"Virika. I have witnessed Ǽcerbot break people of their idealism and sense of justice. Then I saw you find meaning and beauty from nothing but pebble etchings and scraps in the dark. That's what the Antilleans need — indomitable hope. I won't take part in destroying that spirit. Not again."

Anger and guilt heaved within Virika. The muscles in her face clenched. Whether she wanted her to or not, Kalima was about to die. She sat next to her on the bed, remembering Whitehall's tortured last moments of ire directed at her — the blood he'd spat at her and how she'd recoiled from him. What if she had stayed and watched? Would he still be alive? Everyone she was close to had been taken away or died. She silenced her inner turmoil and focused on Kalima's final moments in front of her.

"What do you need from me, Kalima?" Her voice broke. "Are you in pain?"

Kalima's pupils had dilated. "I'm tired. Hold my hand and tell me the best memory you have from when you were a child."

The question softened Virika's anger. "Lie down." She helped Kalima ease back onto the mattress and held her hand like she'd asked. "When I was little on Orinoco, we didn't go on vacation much. Most of our holidays were spent camping outside of Sando, in the province. You know Antilleans love the outdoors." She smiled thinly. "I'd play with other kids and eat a lot. Once, when Daddy was off from the mines, we went on a trip to the coast. The beach was sandy and warm, and Ma had made a picnic. Daddy hadn't told us why he chose that specific spot. But on that beach and only at that time of year, the salabars return to the same place they were born to lay their eggs." She paused. Kalima breathed heavily but nodded. "The little salabars hatch and scurry into the water before they are eaten by vultures. Heh. They're born running from dangers they don't even understand. They spend years out at sea exiled because the beach, their home, isn't safe. And yet, they always remember where they were born. It's part of the very fibre of what makes them up, even though they've barely spent an hour of their lives on that patch of sand. They're always connected to it. We saw them leave, knowing they'd come home one day in the future."

"Perhaps I am going home after wandering the sea," Kalima said. "I hope I remember it when I get there."

Virika brushed the hair from Kalima's forehead. "You will."

Kalima's breath slowed further. She descended into what appeared to be sleep. Virika stayed beside her, holding her until Kalima's chest stopped rising and her pulse ceased. The stillness in the room rushed over her. The sorrow of being completely alone needled her again.

Virika hugged Kalima on the prison cot as tightly as if she were a life raft. Then she undressed her carefully, down to her underwear, folded her uniform, and put it in a corner of the cell along with the locust mask. She gripped Kalima's right hand and held it upward so the blood would pool towards Kalima's elbow, then lowered her hand again. Taking a deep breath, she clamped her lips together, reached for the hacksaw and cut Kalima's hand off just above the wrist. She let the blood from the hand drain into the toilet and then placed it on the floor. Picking up the hacksaw again, she did as Kalima instructed and cut up pieces of the canvas bag. She wrapped the amputated hand inside them, all the while holding back the scream that wanted to rip out of her mouth over the desecration she was committing.

Despite what Virika had done to Kalima's body, she could not leave her naked. Virika dressed Kalima in her discarded prison uniform. She wiped the blood from herself with another piece of cloth and dressed in Kalima's guard uniform. She then donned the locust mask. Her heart thudded as she closed the door behind her using Kalima's palm. When the light came on in Toussard's old cell, it would be time for the early morning shift change. She rested her head against the door to mentally prepare herself. She was about to die. There was no stopping now that Kalima's plan had been set in motion.

"Thank you," she whispered to the door the moment the light flicked on in Toussard's cell.

Straightening her posture, she emulated Kalima's gait. At the end of the corridor, she pressed Kalima's palm flat on the bio-lock. The door slid open and a thrill shot through her. Virika began to climb the stairs, nine flights to the mouth of the Pit. Fear thrummed her pulse louder with each step.

When she reached the final door at the summit, her stomach wrung with fear. Her hands shook as she pressed Kalima's palm to the pad. The door opened. She quickly re-wrapped the hand in the bundle of cloth, set her shoulders back, and walked into the keep. The locusts at the central desk barely registered her entrance — not one of them glanced up. She walked to another door directly opposite the iron gate she'd entered when she'd been processed years ago and unlocked it, her body blocking the guards' view of the severed hand. The door clicked. Fear jolted like electricity through her.

"See you tomorrow, Kalima!" one of the locusts called. Virika waved backwards to acknowledge them and stepped out into the courtyard. How many times had she circuited the keep? The gravel shifting beneath her feet had once been her only source of joy, allowing her to scratch a fleeting moment of freedom into her cell's floor.

The sun had not risen yet. The air was cool and dry. In all her time in the Pit, she'd never been out at night. Beyond the floodlights of the courtyard, she could see the shadows of the guards on watch tracking her. Past the walls, there was the endless black sky with its moon gleaming like a violet disc. She walked across the courtyard, mimicking Kalima's smooth, even strides. The distance from the keep to the rear outer gate stretched for what felt like ages. With each step she braced for a bullet to her chest. When she reached the gate, she pressed Kalima's palm once more into the bio-lock. The gate opened onto the vast desert. She leaned against the wall in shadow before stepping through it.

"My vech is the colour of the sky," she remembered Kalima telling her. She found the lavender vech in the fragile moonlight, put the bundled hand into the storage compartment where Kalima had stowed all of the supplies Virika would need, and punched in the start code. The machine jumped to life beneath her. Her chest tightened as she revved the engine. Exhaust in the air and on her tongue reminded her of being dragged across the sand with Tanager tied to her. He'd been so naive. She wasn't sure whether she wished he was still alive at the bottom of his side of the Pit or that he'd been freed by death.

She slowly circled out of the line of parked vechs, frantic she'd be shot in the head. Kalima's locust mask hid the grimace contorting Virika's lips. She never imagined she'd be thankful for the blank-eyed symbol of her torment. Using the stars as a compass, she oriented herself in the direction of the civilian spaceport, the violet moon at her left, and sped off across the sand.

The expanse surrounding her robbed her of breath. Freedom of movement after being confined for years was disorienting. She did not dare look back or lift her mask, though she wanted to stop and scream into the dark — scream for all the time she'd lost and for her broken heart. As soon as the locusts discovered Kalima's body, they'd be after her. She needed to be gone before they noticed her morning meal was left uneaten.

She did stop, however, somewhere near the midpoint of her drive. She glanced all around her before dismounting and then removed Kalima's hand from the storage compartment and dug a small hole in the loose sandy dirt with her hands. When she was finished digging the small grave, she held Kalima's hand in her own like she had done before Kalima died.

"I understand now. I won't forget you." She kissed Kalima's palm and buried it. She sat there a moment letting her tears soak the sand.

Kalima's directions were exact. Virika found the spaceport and hangars a few hours' drive east through the desert. It was still early and there were few people around the airfield and the outbuildings. She parked Kalima's vech in one of the employee parking zones.

This civilian port was nothing like the desolate patch of sand she and Tanager had been dumped on. It was used mostly to monitor and keep interplanetary travel between Vantalus and Tintaris orderly. The comings and goings were business or industry related. Tintaris was the opposite of a luxury vacation destination. The entire planet served as a manufacturing and prison hub with industries built to keep their workers and families living, Kalima had explained. Cargo could be shipped and citizens were free to travel between the two planets, to visit relatives and find work.

The port night guard was still on shift despite the sun being up. Virika crouched behind a storage building until they'd passed by on their vechs. Her legs verged on cramping. Ducking as she moved, she ran to Hangar C and punched in the code Kalima had made her memorize to gain entrance.

At the far end of the cavernous building were the personal interplanetary ships, PIPs as they called them in the marines. Virika had learned to fly them in the academy, back at the start of her training. She entered the authorization code for PIP 5467 and its cockpit door opened. Kalima had arranged it all: scheduled the personal flight for this morning and booked and paid for the PIP. Virika couldn't believe the outrageous plan Kalima put in place had gone so smoothly. All she had to do was make for the neutral zone beyond Æcerbot space and she would no longer be under their jurisdiction.

"Head for Serth, a dwarf planet outpost for the Kaspan. They won't hand you over to Æcerbot. It's a shared system. The tech and military presence is basic at best." She wished

Kalima were here to witness her hard work come to fruition. That she were alive so Virika could hug her and tell her she was sorry for ever doubting her.

Virika's head grew heavy as she sat in the comfortable cockpit chair. The adrenaline of her flight and escape had run out. She huddled low and tried to sleep. There was still time before the departure slot Kalima had booked.

The clank of the heavy hangar doors opening woke her. Purple shafts of light pierced the cockpit. Still keeping low, Virika watched the coming and going of the maintenance staff. Another small craft from the row across from her slowly taxied out of the hangar and headed to the airfield.

She shut her eyes tight for a moment. It was time. Fingers trembling, she punched in the code Kalima had given her, flipped on the PIP's systems, and navigated out the hangar doors. Few craft were on the airfield at this hour. Perhaps the day would see more steady traffic later. She strapped in and taxied towards the liftoff area.

"Vessel 5467 PIP," a voice crackled over her com. "We've received a bulletin from the Justice Department. All interplanetary flights are grounded until further notice. There's been a breach at the Pit." Virika's heart thundered. PIPs didn't need much space for takeoff. She continued to the liftoff pad.

"Vessel 5467, return to dock at once. You are in violation of code —"

Virika hit the boosters and rocketed upward.

"Dock at once on notice of criminal charges —" Virika ignored the order. They'd found Kalima lying dead on her old prison cot.

"Success or perish," she said to herself. She pushed the PIP to its limit to escape Tintaris's airspace as quickly as she could. As the planet diminished beneath her, her radar picked up a larger craft in pursuit. Her breathing came hard. She had to keep going. It was either outrun these pigs or be thrown into a deeper pit and killed — that is, if they didn't obliterate her in space.

She shut all auxiliary systems and diverted every drop of power to propulsion. The patrol ship was gaining on her. She strapped in and cut a sharp ninety-degree angle. When the craft followed, she plunged downwards, towards the planet. They were faster than her tiny PIP. She could outmanoeuvre them for a short time, but they were closing in and would overtake her well before she reached Serth and Kaspan twenty-five minutes away.

A voice broke into the cockpit: "Virika Sameroo, by the authority of the Æcerbot Empire, we charge you with the murder of Kalima Jackson, theft of an Empire vehicle, and jailbreak. Surrender now and face justice for these charges. If you resist, we will open fire —"

"Shove your trials and charges," Virika said before flicking off all com frequencies. She veered a tight right and then manoeuvred out of their firing range. She couldn't keep pushing the craft to this extreme; at some point she would spin out of control.

A beep alerted her to another large ship at the edge of her radar. She flicked on the com again. No Æcerbot-identifying hail came from its direction. Who would venture so far into Æcerbot territory beyond the buffer zone? With no other option, she gunned for the vessel, zigging and zagging erratically so that the patrol could not target her. She was sorry for whoever she was bringing Æcerbot vengeance down upon. She'd risk these strangers' anger over her own certain death.

Sweat dripped down her forehead. She wiped it away with the back of her hand. She gained a visual of the vessel. It was a privateer cruiser outfitted with firepower beyond its class. She was sure they'd spotted both her and the patroller. The heavily armed ship reoriented itself in the direction Virika was spiralling away from. She checked her radar — the Æcerbot patroller was falling back.

She flipped through the com channels and found the frequency in time to overhear the conversation between the new armed vessel and the patroller.

"This is the Captain of the *Pomerac*. Identify your purpose at this close range to the buffer zone."

"We don't answer to your kind of riffraff. You are beyond the buffer zone and impeding an official mission to retrieve an escaped convict of the Æcerbot Empire. Stand down or you will be deemed an accomplice."

"An Æcerbot convict? The enemy of my enemy is my friend." Laughter from the *Pomerac* filled the channel. "We are granting sanctuary to the craft."

"We will consider this an act of war."

"Don't you consider everything you don't control an act of war? This pilot escaped the Pit with a pathetic ship and got all the way to the buffer zone by themselves with you incompetents unable to catch them? I want to meet this rebel who runs circles around your superior fleet-trained crew. Stand down or we'll make space rain out of you." The laugh had vanished. The captain of the *Pomerac*'s voice had gone tungsten hard.

During the conversation, Virika entered the range of the cruiser. There was nowhere to run from the privateers here. She hovered near the vessel, while the captains of the larger ships postured and flexed, attempting to intimidate each other.

"Æcerbot swine, you have until the count of five to retreat," the *Pomerac*'s captain threatened. "One . . . two . . . three . . ."

Virika screamed in the cockpit. She did not want to be caught in this crossfire with neither side having a stake in keeping her alive. She gasped moments later when the patroller retreated again on the radar.

"Captain of the *Pomerac*," a voice fired across the com. "Vacate Æcerbot territory at once. Warships are on —"

"We'll pick up our guest and be on our way before the lumbering tectonic plate that you call a warship even lifts off." The captain's cocky laugh resurfaced. Virika relaxed her grip on the stick.

Out of prison and into the hands of lawless merce-naries. There was no way of telling whether her situation had improved or worsened, but she was alive for now, if not yet free.

"Well then, escaped Æcerbot convict," the captain of the *Pomerac* hailed in his honey-smooth voice. "I would consider it a personal favour if you'd dock and come aboard. After all, I've saved your life."

Virika gritted her teeth. This wasn't a request for a favour. The ship in front of her could annihilate her in five breaths if she refused. She navigated the PIP alongside it and readied for the confrontation to come.

# SEVEN

# THE POMERAC

A rmed privateers dressed in black uniforms met Virika in the docking bay, stun guns pointed at her chest. Every nerve in her body coiled at the memory of being dragged from her mother's apartment in Paria. None of the armed crew reached out to touch her. She nodded at them curtly and put her hands in the air, stepping forward so they could surround her.

They led her into a lift. After a quick ride up, the doors opened onto a wide, sleek-looking room with the pelican emblem of the rebellion embossed on the far wall. Sitting in the centre, at the head of a polished black table, was a man. He was on the younger end of middle-aged, with dark brown skin and a salt-and-pepper beard. He arched an eyebrow at her.

"I know you, troublesome pilot!" His laugh animated his entire face. "I don't believe in coincidence," he continued. "What are the chances we'd be passing through wretched Æcerbot space at the precise moment you escaped?" He laughed again. "That is what old Antilleans call 'karma.'"

She ignored his laughter. Kept her face impassive as she scrutinized his features. He did look familiar. The shape of his eyes and the swell of his mouth. She knew him, too. He hadn't had the beard back on Icacos.

"You're the captain of the *Calabash*. You accosted me. Æcerbot used the iridium coin you flung at me to convict me of treason." Laughter continued to brighten his face as she seethed.

"Tough talk for a guest on my ship. Was I wrong about how Invictans saw you?" He poured himself a drink from a silver carafe in front of him. "You and I both know you were devoutly loyal to them. What did they do the first chance they got?" He held his palms up. "Charge you with treason and threw you in a hole on Tintaris?"

Virika looked askance. She chewed her cheek; she could not argue with him. "Thank you for saving me."

"You're quite welcome. So, what shall we call you, former Captain of the *Oestra*?"

"Virika Sameroo."

"Sameroo? Exterran Antillean, as I guessed years ago." He slapped the table in front of him.

"My parents won the immigration lottery and we left the mines on Orinoco when I was a child." She interlaced her hands in front of her.

"And how is your allegiance to the Æcerbot Empire now? How do you like their civilized justice and order?" He leaned back in his chair and took a swig from the heavy chalice in front of him.

Virika's hands balled into fists. She fumed at the thought of Lyric advancing up the ranks, of every official who'd turned their back on her. The captain nodded.

"Exactly. No matter how much you loved their Empire, no matter the amount of their doctrine you ate, you were never one of them. You will never be." He shook his head. "Here, sit, have a drink." He motioned to a tall and strapping privateer behind her to bring her a glass. She sat a few seats away from the captain, to his right.

"Thank you." She gulped the pomegranate-flavoured alcohol greedily. She couldn't recall the last time she'd had a drink. The buzz from the liquor hitting her empty stomach was immediate. She found herself smiling at the captain in spite of herself. "What shall I call you?"

"I am Davedeo and you are aboard my ship, the *Pomerac*. I've upgraded from the *Calabash* since we last encountered each other." He grinned, wide and warm. "When's the last time you had some home food?"

"I stopped keeping track of how many days I'd been locked up after a year," she answered. "The last time I ate my mother's cooking was the night before I was arrested just after I'd returned from Icacos."

"That was almost a decade ago." He clucked his tongue. "Phillips!" He called the crewman who'd brought Virika the glass. "See if Dominique has any food on hand. A roti or a curry for Sameroo here." Virika's stomach growled, demanding attention. When Phillips left, Davedeo leaned towards her. "After you've eaten, I have an offer for you, Sameroo. I always knew you had the blood of a renegade. Even back then when you were a little Æcerbot-washed jerk."

She laughed giddily, despite herself. A woman wearing a navy dress that flowed over her full figure entered the room carrying two plates of heavenly scented food. Virika salivated at the meal placed in front of her. Blood rushed to her face. The beautiful, brown-skinned woman made Virika's abdomen quiver. She thought this part of her had petrified after losing Alba. She stared in open admiration.

"Thank you, Dominique." Davedeo held back from laughing at Virika, who seemed to have forgotten how to use words.

Dominique nodded at her. "You ever met a Bequian, let alone have one cook for you?"

"N-no," Virika stuttered.

Dominique laughed. "You've got an Invictan accent and you're about to get an education," she said before leaving the room. Virika smiled in spite of herself.

"Would you like to join my crew, Sameroo? We could use someone with inside knowledge of Invictan and Æcerbot systems and protocol." Davedeo asked after she'd gorged herself on a plate of garlic aloo choka and sada roti so painfully delicious that she'd licked up every drop of oil with her tongue.

She placed both hands flat on the table, hoping to anchor the unease tossing within her. There was nowhere else for her to go. Davedeo and his crew were Antillean, but not like her parents or her community in Paria, or even the family they'd lost contact with in the Antilles. Her education and training had labelled Davedeo and his lot criminals and outlaws, in direct opposition to the civilized order upheld by Æcerbot. Members of this very ship and others like it had attacked Æcerbot transports, stolen cargo, and murdered merchant marines. But wasn't she an escaped convict and murder suspect, too?

"Is this a real choice?" she asked.

"We can set you down on Icacos, on any one of the neutral zone planets to fend for yourself." He paused. "I know what you've been told about us, about yourself and who you are. Some of the violence attributed to us is true. I cannot lie. Get that education Dominque mentioned and judge for yourself. Any one of my crew is free to leave at any time. There are no prisoners on my ship."

Virika nodded. She would remain onboard for the time being, if only to eat more of Dominque's cooking.

Sixty days later, Davedeo caught word that the Æcerbot tramp ship *Carrick* would call at Arsc on Elistal on the edge of Gaul space for three days. He rubbed his chin at the great table where the entire crew, including Virika, were assembled for their evening meal. She ate in silence, relishing the spiced pickled mango on her plate and absorbing the chatter around her. The crew, who had since taken to her, hailed from across the Exterran Antilles: Davedeo, from Iyonola, and Phillips, from Chantimelle, had as young men joined Toussard's cause just before the rebellion was crushed. They'd escaped detection but refused to return to work in the Æcerbot-dependent industries on their respective planets. Everyone aboard the *Pomerac* — Aria, Johns, Jacobs, Dass, all of them — and the crews of nearly every other privateering ship had had direct or indirect ties to Toussard or had taken inspiration from him. Dominique, who had witnessed the rebellion on Bequia as a teenager, had explained all this to Virika.

"'Once you taste freedom, once you recognize the gruel they've forced you to subsist on for their benefit, you will never swallow it willingly again,' I heard Toussard say in a speech."

"Is that why you like cooking?" Virika had asked her.

"Partly." She'd smiled. "My father was Toussard's second-in-command. Sometimes, it's safer if I remain on the ship."

"There must be valuable cargo aboard if the *Carrick* doesn't want to dally on sleepy Elistal so far out from the usual routes," Davedeo mused at the table.

"There's an outbreak of a fever on Elistal," Phillips said between mouthfuls of curry. He was a cheerful yet physically intimidating man. "Maybe they don't want to pick up the germ?"

Virika almost choked at the mention of the fevers. She never wanted to witness the nightmare they wreaked on anyone again.

"Dominique," Phillips continued, "this is almost as good as what you could buy on Chantimelle. *Almost*. It needs more pepper." Dominque pretended to be offended at his good-natured teasing. Virika managed to catch her eye.

*The food's delicious*, she mouthed towards her. Her stomach fluttered at the smile illuminating Dominique's face. She wanted to make Dominique smile often. Aria and Johns glanced at each other before bursting into laughter.

"Why don't you two stop playing and start sharing a bunk." Johns smirked.

Aria slapped him gently on the shoulder. "Johns. You

don't have to say it out loud." She glanced at Dominique. "He's right though," she added laughing.

"The fevers. They might help us," Virika heard Davedeo say. She nodded as she attempted to keep herself from smiling.

Virika followed Phillips and a squad of six *Pomerac* crew, masked and garbed in blue medic uniforms, through the crowded air dockyard of Arsc. It was early morning and her stomach leapt at the fresh baked bread-scented air. Yard workers and automated dock receivers were busy loading and unloading cargo from transport ships. No one took notice of what appeared to be a routine health inspection crew. As they neared the *Carrick*, Phillips wielded the forged paperwork that would permit them to board the ship for a mandatory health assessment. The ship's scheduled inspection, Davedeo's contacts had learned, would occur three hours later. The *Pomerac*'s crew had to convince the *Carrick*'s officers that the inspectors had arrived early. Virika, who'd handled boarding permits while stationed aboard the *Oestra*, forged the document herself at a print shop in the adjacent town of Frith.

"Art school was worth every sovereign," she said when she'd shown her handiwork to Davedeo.

"You recreated the Ministry's seal in the exact lavender ink," Davedeo remarked. She'd puffed up with pride.

Now, as the squad drew near their target, sweat pooled on her upper lip. Her breath was short and shallow. She forced herself to move forward despite her legs wanting to tear off in the opposite direction of any Æcerbot official. It was as if the unyielding gaze of the locusts were upon her again, like she was marching back into the Pit. She shifted her mask, wiped her mouth, and kept moving.

The raid was her first, and a test of her commitment to Davedeo and her new crewmates. She'd shared all she knew about trade routes and protocols, but she still had to pull her physical weight on the *Pomerac* despite the warmth of its camaraderie. Get her hands dirty. That meant subduing and attacking Æcerbot or other official personnel. Regardless of her desire to rip the Empire apart with her bare hands, a lingering reverence for the tan and red-accented uniform rankled her like an infected wound. The uniform had symbolized safety, progress, and hope for her family. Even after torture and grief, an upswell of devotion stirred within her at the sight of it.

"You're early." The first lieutenant of the *Carrick*'s granite-hard voice broke through Virika's thoughts. "Elistal hires you dogs to do its testing?" She looked up, stunned, while he scrutinized their paperwork in front of the hatch. She'd been called slurs in whispers at the academy and openly while in the Pit but never in broad daylight. Behind them the docks grew noisy with increased traffic. Hopefully this would conceal the other members of the crew poised to provide cover fire nearby.

Phillips stooped, ignoring the remark. "We had a cancellation."

Mollified, the lieutenant wrinkled his nose and gave them entry. Virika lowered her head as he walked them through the familiar ship layout on their way to the bridge and the captain there. Though the lower portion of her face was hidden by her mask, she didn't want to run the risk of anyone recognizing her as an escaped Pit inmate.

"Let's get this over with," the captain said when they entered the bridge, barely acknowledging the *Pomerac* crew. Phillips positioned himself in front of the wiry man. "We haven't left the ship, any of us. This is a waste of time and resources." He wasn't a captain that Virika had met before; most likely he'd been commissioned while she was locked away. Life had gone on in the Empire without her — her absence hadn't caused a divot in Æcerbot's existence.

"Have a seat, Captain," Phillips directed. Virika and the other privateers fanned out about the bridge to attend to the other officers and wait for the signal. She stood in front of the engineering console, pretending to prep a swab for the engineer's throat.

"Now, Captain," Phillips said slowly. *"Hold still."*

Virika grabbed a knife from her kit and pressed it up against the engineer's neck. Hands trembling, she fought the urge to lower the blade away from the man's artery. Long ago, she'd sworn an oath to protect men like the uniformed engineer in front of her.

"Secure the hatch and the entire ship," she ordered. Her knees went weak. She'd become the thief and criminal that her parents, who'd been the perfect immigrants, scorned. Shame pressed like a boulder against her chest. She glanced towards Phillips for reassurance. Ten years ago, Virika could have been in the same position as the crewmen before her. The engineer, taking advantage of her distraction, shifted towards the console and jabbed his elbow into her ribs. *Crack.* She doubled over and grabbed her side as she stabbed him in the small of his back. Recovering, she pulled the knife out and pushed it up against his carotid. Blood dripped onto his lapel. She hadn't wanted to hurt him. Guilt sickened her.

"Secure the ship or I'll slit your throat and secure it myself," she said, holding back a gasp of pain.

Phillips and the others relieved the ship's small crew of their guns and rounded up the captain and other personnel in the centre of the bridge. When she was sure the engineer had locked down the vessel's hatches, she shoved him, bleeding, towards his fellow crewmates.

"Hands up. You've done a fabulous job making this easy for us *dogs*. Let's keep up the good work." Phillips motioned to Dass. "You and I will stay here. The rest of you, get to the cargo bay and off-load."

"Antillean trash," the captain spat before a blunt *thwack* silenced him. Virika led the others to the hold. The space was filled with the usual cargo a light freighter would take on, but nothing to warrant the haste with which the *Carrick* wanted to depart.

"There's nothing here," Aria said. Virika motioned the unit to the perimeter of the hold. "Smaller ships like this one have a concealed compartment where the crew stores valuable goods. Run your hands along the walls; see if you can find it." Virika leaned forward to catch her breath. The jabbing pain in her ribs was slowing her down. If they couldn't find the cache quickly, the raid would be a waste.

"Here," Johns called. They all hurried over to where he was standing in front of what looked like a large locker door that he'd propped open. Inside was a crate marked *Rh*.

"Is that all?" Aria threw her hands up.

"It's rhodium," Virika said in disbelief. "This crate is all we need. One of you, go back to the bridge and tell Phillips we're exiting. If the other two can lift this crate, we'll get the captain to override the hatch and stroll out of here."

She led them to the exit. Phillips and Dass, along with the other crewman, were making their way along the corridor towards them. The captain of the *Carrick*, whose lip was swollen, walked ahead of them awkwardly as if something sharp was pointed at his back.

"Open the hatch," Phillips ordered. The captain squinted at Virika.

"I've seen your face somewhe—" Phillips knocked him upside his head. Virika's chin dropped to her chest. The captain swayed as he punched in the code near the door. It lowered in front of them.

"Good," Phillips said. "Once we're out, shut it again. We've men posted around the port. If you end up shot, it will be for not locking down like I told you."

The *Pomerac* crew bolted out into the dockyard. Virika ran, teeth gritted against the knifing pain. Laser fire shot across the dock, coming from the unclosed hatch. Chaos erupted as everyone screamed, ducked, and dashed for cover.

She, Aria, and Dass split off from the rest of the unit, taking a separate route to the back room of the Heretic Pub in an unsavoury part of town. Virika could barely keep up. Footsteps thundered after them through Arsc's winding streets. She was on the verge of collapse when Dass yanked her by her collar.

"In here," he whispered. They hid in a frightened old man's bakery stall until she'd caught her breath, then cautiously snuck back to the meeting point. When Phillips let them into the room of the Heretic, all accounted for, Virika hugged Aria and burst into tears.

"You did it!" Aria hugged Virika back. Two hours later they'd returned to the *Pomerac* via forged medical inspection certificates and were speeding away from Elistal as quickly as they could.

"That was easier than expected," Phillips laughed. They all were seated at the communal table for dinner with Davedeo.

"No one expects a raid on Elistal. They'll be prepared next time." He eyed Virika, who'd been favouring her left side all evening. "It seems the job was easier for some of you than others."

She curled her shoulders inward. "I'm told you let your guard down," he said. She looked at her plate, heat rushing to her face. She'd let old loyalties cloud her focus. "Never trust an Empire official, even when you have a knife against their throat." Davedeo rubbed his chin.

"Go easy on her, Davedeo." Dominique pulled a chair out to sit next to Virika. Mischief beat in her musical voice; the tension lifted. "The rhodium she identified has made us richer and will help our interests throughout the Antilles." She put her hand on Virika's forearm. "How about I take a look at that sore rib?" She winked, though concern coloured her slick talk.

"You're the cook and the ship's medic?" Virika waggled her eyebrows at Dominique.

"For you?" She lowered her voice. "I can be anything."

Virika gulped.

"If you'll excuse us, Captain," she said, pushing her seat back. Aria and Johns both smiled while keeping their eyes on their plates. Virika wanted to escape Davedeo's reprimand as much as she wanted to be Dominique's patient. "We'll be in my quarters."

Phillips laughed as Virika exited the dining hall with Dominique close behind.

Davedeo arranged for the sale of the rhodium to a Gaulish buyer and split the profits among the crew and himself, keeping some to distribute among their contacts in the Antilles.

"Here's your portion." He counted out a large stack of sovereigns and slid them over to Virika.

"What?" She clapped a hand to her cheeks. It was enough for her and her mother to live on in Paria for two full years. When they next stopped in Icacos, Virika acquired paint, charcoal, and canvas with a tiny portion of the money.

She covered the walls of her cabin with sketches of her mother and Alba. She longed to see their faces, but how could she attempt to return to Invicta to search for them with a warrant and a bounty on her head? She drew a picture of Kalima on the wall next to her bed. Every night she thanked her for her freedom before she fell asleep.

Her tactical expertise and knowledge of vessels proved invaluable in outmanoeuvring faster and better-armed Æcerbot convoys when the *Pomerac* was chased near skip gates or from within Empire space. Gaining Davedeo's trust, she climbed the informal ranks quickly, her pockets filling and her network of privateers and sympathizers growing.

All the while Virika laughed and learned the culture she'd been denied on Invicta from her newfound family. Phillips feted with her for carnival in lavish costumes on Chantimelle. Davedeo took them all swimming in the Orange Sea on Iyonola. Aria and Johns became the silly siblings she never had. And Dominique, who was the heart of the ship, served up delicacies that revived Virika's atrophied taste buds and soothed her troubled soul, kissing her tears away.

She took in everything, including the struggle, poverty, and ill health the constant physical work in the fields or mines wreaked on the Antilleans. Despite the joys they'd carved out for themselves, they were not free. They lived and died producing what the empires needed at subsistence wages. She wanted to remain among them.

Toussard's cache of iridium hidden on lonely Bocas, coupled with Kalima's death, clawed at the heart of Virika's newfound happiness. Such thoughts fanned her desire for justice, which threatened to cool with time and kindness. She wrestled with the choice to forget her past and erase it from her mind like the locusts had done with her etchings on her cell floor. Her duty to her mother, her father's memory, Whitehall's honour, Kalima's last wishes, and most of all her people's struggle across the Æcerbot Empire marred every joyous moment with sorrow. The seductive tug of adventuring and shore leave in resort towns, passing the rest of her life in luxury with Dominique in her arms, was intoxicating.

"You haven't hurt anyone," Dominique whispered, one night when Virika woke in their shared bunk, convinced she'd murdered everyone on the *Pomerac*. She traced her finger down Dominique's thigh.

"I can't stay," Virika said. Her hair had grown back and her cheeks had filled out again but guilt simmered in her gut.

Dominique brushed the hair from Virika's brow. "Can I come with you?"

"I don't know if I'll succeed or survive what I have to do."

"I won't let you do this alone," Dominique whispered.

"What did I do to deserve you?" She smiled.

"Who says you deserve me?" Dominique squeezed her tight.

"Davedeo?" She sat with him on the beach on the resort planet Troumaca, at the edge of the neutral trade zone. "I want leave to seek my own justice for what's been done to me. I'm grateful for the harbour you've given me on the *Pomerac*. But I can't live not knowing what's become of my mother and those I loved back on Invicta."

"You won't like what you find, Virika." He did not grin like he had at their first meeting. His voice was gravelly and sombre. He rubbed his hand over his chin. "We privateers have kept the resistance alive. You will hear even Antilleans say we are lawless, violent, and greedy — that we threaten stability, commerce, and peace. But Phillips, myself, Dominique, Dass, Aria, Johns, the crews of the other ships, we were there when Toussard asked for better wages, better living conditions, and for part of the profits from our labour to be reinvested into the Antilles peacefully instead of syphoned away and rationed back to our powerless elected governments. We were there when he was denied. We were there when Bequia's revolution was crushed and our families and innocent people were killed. We are the only alternative, but our people are not ready. They are afraid and do not see that Æcerbot will never treat us with respect or dignity willingly."

"They locked me in a hole and left me there to lose my mind." The sea sparkled front of them. It reminded her of the beach on Orinoco where she'd seen the little salabars hatch as a girl. "I have lost everything I loved. I was utterly alone in the dark. I am not a green merchant marine recruit. What more can they take from me? I know the horror buried at the foundation of the Empire. I am not afraid of Invicta."

Davedeo nodded, though Virika could tell he was unconvinced.

"All right, Sameroo. You don't need my leave or my blessing, but you have both. You *have* come a long way from the ignorant fool you were all those years ago on Icacos." He extended his hand to shake hers. She reached out but pulled her hand back at the last moment.

"Dominique is leaving with me." She laughed. Davedeo rolled his eyes and slapped the table with his palm.

"Come on, Virika, be reasonable. I lose the best of my crew *and* the only person on board this ship who can make roti as soft as a cloud. Are you trying to kill me?" His twinkling smile returned with an edge of sadness.

"You'll find someone who cooks as well as her." She shrugged and grinned, knowing it was Dominique's spirit that Davedeo and the crew would miss most.

"I will not! But be on your way before I get hungry and change my mind."

This time Virika seized his hand and shook it gratefully.

# EIGHT

# BOCAS

Virika and Dominique left Troumaca in a PIP they bought with money they'd earned from plundering. Together they made their way to Orinoco, the planet of Virika's birth. They holed up in a hotel there in the vibrant capital, Sando, amassing the supplies they needed to make the trek to Bocas.

The current Æcerbot presence in the Exterran Antilles was minimal. With no threat of insurgence, the ability to amass a large military force in the star system quickly, and the planetary self-governments subservient to Empire mining interests, Invictan officials had relaxed their surveillance of the Antilleans. Virika blended into the population without much worry of capture.

The streets of Sando teemed with people and beat with a pulse more vital than what she'd experienced in Paria. Fleeting images of picnics in the hibiscus-scented capital gardens and strolls along the busy city boardwalk came to her unbidden when she stared out across the stone buildings of the planet's administrative centre.

Beyond the capital, crushing poverty and desperation shackled the citizens of Orinoco. She caught bars of long-forgotten melodies on the lips of tired women wandering the crowded market. They sang of toil and grief, loss and hope. She tried to hold these memories fast, but her grasp of her early years was tenuous. The accents and flavours were her own and yet not. The Orinoco that lived inside her was not the one that lived and struggled today. She and her parents were a relic, a time capsule of the place they'd left, untouched by the film of mine dust that settled on every surface.

Virika, though she revelled in every moment of her reconnection, found herself out of sync with the place of her birth.

Her ties to her extended family had been severed. Visits to Invicta weren't permitted and money could not be sent back home to families in the Antilles. She could only remember the familiar names she called her grandmother, aunts, and uncles. Her parents had never taught her the official ones. She and Dominique had no time in their itinerary to do a thorough search for any of them. Sameroo was a rare-enough surname and any inquiries might arouse suspicion among the few local Æcerbot officials. And what if she were able to locate her family, would they remember her? Would they welcome her, or would they view her mother and father as traitors? Sellouts who left the family behind for their own betterment without a thought to the people who'd nurtured them?

Virika would never be fully Antillean, regardless of what Davedeo had proclaimed her to be or how open

Orinoco's people were in spite of the arduous mining work that ground them down at an early age. She belonged nowhere now, except with Dominique.

Within a week, they'd procured the survival equipment and arms they'd need for Bocas. The planet was three days' travel from Bequia, Dominque's birthplace and the heart of Toussard's rebellion. They spent two nights in the city of Nova, on Bequia, to reset and regroup. The little planet still bore the scars of Toussard's shattered rebellion. Deep cracks remained in the facades of the administrative buildings, which looked to be on the verge of collapse. Dominque's joy vanished and a wounded expression mirroring Nova's derelict cities possessed her face. Bequia's people were flinty. When Virika, who stuck out as a foreigner, said, "Hello," or spoke to them, the Bequians acted as if Virika had cursed them.

"We don't trust foreigners or those who consort with them," yelled an old man sitting on the steps of a dilapidated church when they asked where they could purchase food stocks.

"We won't find help here," Dominique said as they headed empty-handed back to their hotel, anguish in her voice. "Too many of the Bequians that remain betrayed Toussard and helped turn in people like my father."

On the morning of their departure, Dominique squeezed Virika's hand as they settled into the PIP to lift off.

"Bocas means 'mouths.' Why do you suppose they called the planet that?"

Virika shrugged. "We're about to find out."

Bocas was exactly as Kalima had described it: a dwarf planet on the outer edge of the habitable planets in the Antillean star system, past the wild habitable worlds Exterran Antillean families visited to camp and fish on their short vacations from the mines. It had been left uninhabited. Still, the fact that not one of the greedy empires felt the land worth pillaging made Virika uneasy. Whenever she or Dominique had mentioned the planet to anyone in Sando, the other person's neck would stiffen. Their joking manner would stutter to a halt, and their demeanour would become as unfriendly as the Bequians'.

"Dat place is not good to visit. It have blight there. Bettah to go Toco or St. George to relax and camp," was the general response. When she tried to probe deeper into the nature of the danger, they'd ended the conversation and walked away.

Bocas appeared, a sphere of green and blue like the pictures of old Terra but with a thin ring around it.

Kalima's words came to mind as their PIP drew nearer to the dreaded planet: there was something alive on Bocas, but Toussard couldn't describe it. He'd told Kalima it hurt everyone differently.

"It's beautiful," Dominique whispered. Virika nodded, panic coalescing beneath her sternum. She focused the PIP's sensors on Bocas's ring, enlarging the visual.

"What is that made out of? It doesn't seem like dust or rock," she wondered, staring at the alabaster oval that circled the planet. Dominique covered her mouth and held her breath a moment before she spoke.

"Are those bones?"

Virika's voice was as heavy as an anvil. "Yes."

They landed the PIP on the blood-coloured beach of a goat-shaped island in Bocas's southern hemisphere. Thick jungle encroached on the sand, and black vulture-like birds roosted in the trees. There were so many of the wretched creatures the branches themselves appeared shrouded in mourning veils. Looking eastward from where they'd landed, Virika could see the red cliffs Kalima had described to her. There was a weight about the air, a foreboding she could not articulate. It made her want to run back into the PIP with Dominique and seal the hatch.

"Stay with the PIP. I'm going to scout the place out. If I don't come back, leave. Don't come after me." Virika's eyes pleaded with Dominique, willing her to agree to her terms.

Dominique put her hand on Virika's shoulder. "I'm not going to leave."

Virika grabbed Dominique and kissed her so hard they stumbled backward against the craft. She let go and plodded off across the beach, occasionally checking back for Dominique, who was busy exploring the shoreline. The sand was heavy and the cliffs off at quite a distance. She pushed on, thinking of Tanager at the bottom of the Pit. Her legs trembled with exhaustion like they had on Tintaris. A humming surrounded her as she neared the caves. She could not make out where the sound originated. It grew louder, reverberating in her head and vibrating her teeth.

*Thirty paces into the smallest mouth*, Kalima had told her. The humming differentiated, separating into distinct voices the closer she came to the entrance of the cave. Her stomach dropped.

They were voices she knew.

*You left me, Viri. I begged you not to join the marines and you left me.*

Her mother's words skewered her.

*You mean that, don't you?*

Her ache for Alba washed over her.

The words *savage slut* slammed into her chest, followed by the laughter of every locust guard in the Pit. The sound assaulted her from every angle. She sat on the rocks by the opening of the cave Kalima had described, the wind knocked out of her.

Bocas *was* cursed. She would go mad if she remained near the caves too long. She couldn't silence the barrage. It was coming from within her. Crystallized guilt and shame and anger shredded her to the quick and drained her of her will.

*How had Toussard withstood the torment to cache his entire hoard here?*

She entered the cavern, sobbing as the voices of her past pierced her heart and bled her. Vision blurred by tears, she came upon a chamber filled with small canisters marked with the Æcerbot seal. She gasped. There was enough iridium here to fund any and all of her endeavours. Enough to ignite a revolt, to set her people against the Empire that had exploited their labour for centuries. The word *dog* broke into her thoughts so abruptly it came as a punch to the stomach. She grasped one of the smallest canisters. She could not withstand staying in the cavern for long.

Every moment of despair she'd ever experienced weighed upon her as she hauled the impossibly heavy canister out of the cave and across the beach to the PIP. The vultures left the trees. Their flapping wings beat along with the merciless recounting of the sins inside her head. She collapsed to her knees in the sand, the buzzards circling overhead like a black cloud swarming, eager to swallow her.

"Vultures! Vultures!" Whitehall had rasped a lifetime ago.

Dominique came running over to her, swiping at the birds with a branch.

"You're okay. I'm here," she panted. "What happened? Was something else in there?" Dominique wiped Virika's tear-streaked face.

"Me," she coughed. "I found myself."

Virika and Dominique alternated dragging one iridium canister at a time out of the cave and back to their PIP. Desolation washed over them each time they neared the mouth. They were only able to perform the task twice a day each before succumbing to convulsive sobs. The retrieval stretched on for four months, each trip inside the cave eating away at their confidence and sense of self. They hadn't brought enough rations for the duration of their stay — Dominique resorted to supplementing their dwindling supply with the bitter plants and rubbery molluscs they scavenged at the mucky edges of the jungle and beach.

Vultures circled overhead, swooping in to peck and gouge at their flesh the moment either let their guard down. *We will die here and our bones by some curse will join the planet's funerary ring*, Virika thought each time she encountered the winged tormentors.

"What do the voices say to you?" she asked one night while huddled in the cockpit, blistered and bleeding as the daylight died.

"I hear my grandmother begging my father in our kitchen: 'Marcus, don't go with Toussard. If yuh love us, yuh would stay here and make sure we safe.' Me, agreeing with her: 'Yeah, Daddy, you don't love us.' Bone-shaking explosions. Children, hungry and crying. Women screaming like the end of the world had arrived. My father in the dark whispering, 'Dominique, I want you to go with Davedeo. You *will* be safe with him.'"

Virika wiped a tear from Dominique's cheek. A pained frown contorted her mouth.

"They also speak in your voice." She exhaled. "You tell me I failed you, like I failed my father."

"You could never fail anyone, Dominique." Virika held Dominique close and closed her eyes as the flap of the vultures' wings engulfed the PIP.

# NINE

# ICACOS

Virika walked through the Icacos market on a breezy late spring afternoon. She wore a white blouse that covered her wrist brand, a tailored red waistcoat and trousers. It was the same garb that many of the affluent who lived on Icacos wore when they went for a stroll around town. Today, though she kept a leisurely pace, there was a direction and purpose to her outing. She was in search of a particular fruit stand at the heart of the market and an old woman selling Tollian mangoes. She'd sent her groundskeeper out weeks earlier to see if the woman still maintained a stall twice a week. She was speechless when she learned the ancient woman still did.

She came upon the stall more quickly than she'd anticipated. Eyeing the plump Tollian mangoes, she thought of how she'd enjoyed them long ago.

"They sweet?" she asked the greyed, hunched-over woman tending the stall. Had her own mother aged as rapidly? Was she bent and weary from sorrow and labour? Virika wondered.

"Sweeta den —" The woman's words withered as she peered at Virika. Her eyes were duller than Virika remembered. "I sorry, madam, lady. I feel I know yuh."

Virika chuckled. "Is that so? What makes you say that?"

"Yuh voice. That wishy-wash accent. I hear it before."

Virika smirked. "Visit my home tonight for dinner. We'll see if we can jog your memory." She handed the woman a card with her address on it. It was in the most affluent district of the port. She took two mangoes from the stand. "I'll pay you for these when I see you tonight." She sauntered off towards the docks, reminiscing about her days on the *Oestra*, back when she thought she'd had the world in the palm of her hands.

"More raids, I see. Tsk tsk," Virika said that evening, scrolling the news on her touchscreen while seated at the table on the terrace. "The Empire seems to be crumbling at its edges, doesn't it?" She winked at Dominique sitting next to her. After months spent removing the iridium from the cave and selling a percentage of it to the Gauls for a fortune, Virika and Dominique had set up house on Icacos to rest and recover from the voices that had haunted them on Bocas.

"Why yes, it does. A pity." Dominique curled her lip. She wore a dusty rose dress that heightened the natural blush in her skin as the sun set. This was in complete contrast to the plain tan-and-red-accented trousers and shirt Virika wore. It recalled her old uniform — she hoped it might help refresh the fruit seller's memory.

The terrace was one of three attached to the expansive whitewashed villa they'd purchased, which was bright and open to the breeze. Virika insisted on large windows and grounds filled with mature trees laden with fruit she could pick and eat whenever she wanted. The two spent most of their time outdoors, enjoying the air and sun that Virika had been denied for so long.

"The Baroness," their valet announced with a smile in his voice. The old woman from the market appeared in a faded flower-print dress. Virika and Dominique stood to greet her.

"Baroness, welcome," Virika said. "Please sit down with us. We were about to have dinner."

The old woman sat across from Virika. Her eyebrows knitted together as she stared. The party remained quiet as valets brought out steaming dhalpuris, curried fish, and a spicy shrimp bujol.

Virika studied the old woman intently. "Do you remember me now?"

The old woman trembled. "Yes. Yuh was a soldier years ago who come to meh stand."

"You have a remarkable memory. Why would you remember a random merchant marine from so many years ago? What about our brief meeting would have created such an indelible memory?" Virika ripped a piece of dhalpuri, which Dominique had helped make, and used it to pick up a shrimp and pop it in her mouth. She wanted to draw the Baroness out, discover whether she'd been part of the conspiracy to have her charged. She savoured the ground cumin in the dhal mixture while waiting for the woman to answer.

The Baroness licked her lips. "I remember yuh because yuh was dee first Antillean in an Æcerbot uniform I ever seen. Since when dey let people like we join dem army? And den right after yuh left meh stall another soldier like yuh came. A big white man with blond hair."

"Lyric." Virika stopped herself from spitting after the name. "Do you remember what he wanted? What did he say about me?"

"He wanted to know what I did give yuh in dee packet."

Virika leaned back and chewed her food thoughtfully. "What was in the packet? You told me not to drink it. Was it poison?"

The corners of the Baroness's lips bent downward. An indignant fire flared across her face. She pulled an identical sachet from the folds of her dress and placed it on the table between them.

"I said a prayers over it. It was a charm. To keep people safe. I had a sense yuh would need protection. When yuh left meh stall, dis Lyric man come and grab meh up and tell meh to give him dee same packet I give yuh. So I did." She touched her neck. "He bruised up meh arms and neck. I didn't come back to dee stall for a couple weeks to make sure all yuh did leave so I didn't have to see he again."

Virika did not touch the packet. She marked the tremor passing through the old woman's lips while she recounted Lyric's treatment of her. Lyric had gotten the envelope and somehow tampered with the packet in evidence. That was the only answer for any poison or illness-inducing substance within it. Virika pursed her lips.

"I believe you, Baroness," she said. "Did you see this soldier afterward? Did he hurt you again?"

The Baroness nodded. "He come back to dee stall again and again over dee years. Roughing me up and never paying. He became captain and den one time he had come for some meeting, he tell me he was a commander. Once I did ask about you, the Antillean soldier I asked for. He laugh and said yuh was a criminal and in a jail on Tintaris."

Virika frowned and poured the woman a drink. "I shall have to pay him a visit. The next time you see an Æcerbot ship docked at port and taking on cargo, send word to me here as soon as you can. Here is the money for your mangoes, and for your trouble." She took five hundred sovereign notes from her pants pocket and handed it to the Baroness.

The Baroness gawked at the money. It was more than she'd make in several seasons at her stall. "Thank you . . . but so much? Why?" she stammered.

"You remind me of someone I love. Keep it, there'll be more when that ship docks."

"Yes, Miss. But what I supposed to call yuh?" Virika smiled at Dominique, who'd been sitting silently throughout the discussion.

"Countess. The Countess of Sando." A gleam shone in Virika's eye. "We're all nobles here, aren't we?"

"To the Countess," Dominique toasted.

"To the Baroness." The Countess raised her glass to their guest and downed her drink.

Word arrived at the villa three weeks later, of an Æcerbot ship, the *Mersea*, docked at port. The Countess had her paid spies tail the crew to learn its captain's habits — what he liked to drink and the dock girls he liked to fuck. She summoned these hard-working women to the villa, where she and Dominique discovered what his penchants were by sampling their services themselves. They paid the women exceptionally well for the privilege.

On a warm evening, the Countess settled into a dark corner of the Gilded Lady. The captain of the *Mersea* paraded inside sometime after dark. She bristled at the man's arrogant swagger. Had she behaved like this? Had she walked into the pub as if she owned it, as if she were made of better mettle than its patrons? She watched him from her shadowy corner, observed as he downed several beers, laughed obnoxiously at his own jokes, and touched the women who brought him his pints without their consent. She caught his eye at one point and beckoned him over. He stood and strutted over to her like a peacock doing her a favour, flashing her a smile as he took the chair across from her.

"You're a little old for me, don't you think?"

She sipped her wine to keep from laughing. "You are very sure of yourself, Captain Horatio Yorkton. An excellent quality in an Æcerbot merchant marine captain."

Despite his slightly inebriated state, his gaze sharpened. "My reputation precedes me. And who are you, lurking in the shadows like a Paria thief?"

"You may call me the Countess of Sando." She poured herself another glass of wine.

"There is no countess of that Antillean hellhole." A sneer jerked his lips. He swigged his beer. The Countess took the insult in stride. "Now, what is it you really want?" He winked at her.

The Countess put her glass down. "I want you to go back to Invicta and deliver a message to the prime minister and the head of the merchant marine. Tell them if they want their ships to pass freely in the trade and neutral zones, they'll agree to a diplomatic meeting with Antillean representatives in neutral territory regarding the standard of living in the Exterran Antilles."

Captain Yorkton scoffed. "I will deliver no such message. The Æcerbot Empire does not strike deals with privateers or trash." He set his shoulders back and puffed out his chest.

The Countess smirked. "All right. I'm commandeering your ship and crew."

Yorkton laughed again and stood up from the table. "See here, Countess whatever. Stop wasting my time. Commandeering the *Mersea* will not break my oath to defend the Empire." He began to walk away.

"What's the name of that dark-haired woman you like at the docks — Vrinda, was it?" She spoke audibly enough for everyone in the inn to hear. He stopped and turned on his heel, returning to the table warily. "Yes, that's it. Vrinda. Mmmm. I like her, too. She does the same routine for me. She's lovely."

Yorkton's face turned beet red.

"Oh, I'd forgotten. That act is taboo on Invicta. Not *illegal*, but it would definitely get you shunned and passed over for promotion." She swirled her wine glass. "I know who of your disgruntled crew would love to have this information regarding our shared kink." She smiled the same hard smile full of hate she'd used as a veneer over her anger her entire life.

Yorkton sat back down and spoke in a gravelly whisper. "What have I done to you for you to jeopardize my livelihood in this manner? I don't even know you." He wiped the perspiration beading at his hairline.

The Countess rolled her eyes. "Yes. That's how it works. You have never physically done harm to me, a savage born in a hellhole. You can dust off your hands and protect your fragile feelings while the Empire you love and protect rapes and pillages people so it can breathe." She hissed the words at him.

Yorkton clenched his jaw.

"Horatio," she said, referring to him by his first name, disregarding his rank and title, "in case you think you might agree to deliver my message but not follow through, know this: my people are everywhere. It'll get back to me if you haven't done what I've asked. I will pay my informant handsomely and they will return with your captainship to Icacos. Further —" she took another sip of her drink "— I will be commandeering half of your ship's cargo as collateral. Your *Empire* may have the rest when you provide me with their affirmative answer. If I do not receive an answer within two months, we'll increase the raids and seize control of the shipping ports. Not one ounce of iridium will pass the skip gates." She stood up, flung a pelican iridium coin on the table as payment for her drinks, and left in a flourish.

By the time she arrived at the villa, she had word that her crew had seized half of the *Mersea*'s cargo, including its entire iridium shipment destined for Invicta. She hummed an old Antillean tune as she settled into bed next to Dominique.

"Let them leave Icacos without agreeing. We'll see if they're foolish enough to think I'm bluffing."

While the Countess waited, she, Davedeo, and her friends on the *Pomerac* sent word to the other privateer captains and their crews of the ultimatum she'd issued. The spirit of Toussard's revolution had never faded among them — they agreed that they would coordinate with the resistance efforts when called upon in exchange for a portion of any plunder taken from intercepted Æcerbot ships and to share strategic intelligence with one another. The ghost of Bequia's derelict streets hung heavy over Dominique, the Countess, and their allies. Whenever the Countess felt her own resolve waiver, she'd close her eyes and repeat Toussard's words, etched into the cell at the bottom of the pit: *Death is better*.

The response from the Empire came two months later: *Invicta does not negotiate with lawless savage pirates.*

The Countess cracked her knuckles and wrote back without hesitation:

*You're cut off.*

Davedeo and his fellow privateer captains focused their raids on all Æcerbot cargo ships at neutral zone trade hubs while permitting the Kaspans and Gauls to transport iridium and other raw materials extracted from the Antillean star system freely. Cargo seized from Æcerbot ships was sold to the Kaspans and Gauls at a discounted price, and part of the profits were shared with the leadership of the planets where Æcerbot held larger commercial interests: Iyonola, Chantimelle, and Orinoco. In turn, the Kaspans aided the privateers with intelligence and raised tariffs on imports of Æcerbot goods. Shared profits with Antilleans allowed the Countess to gain an audience with the Exterran Antillean representatives: Laurette Vincent of Chantimelle, Martin Hernandez of Iyonola, and Ben Ram of Orinoco. She, Dominique, and Captain Davedeo held a summit for them aboard the *Pomerac*.

"This money is only scraps of what you are owed," the Countess told those assembled in the ship's dining room. "You must be unified in your economic resistance if you are to secure a better life for your people. You cannot leave your fate to the whims of the empires." There were nods about the table but no commitments.

Laurette spoke up: "Our major industry is fibres for fabrics. The cloth for every tunic worn by an Invictan is produced on Chantimelle. We don't have as large a mining sector as Orinoco or Bequia. What do we have to gain? Why endanger the stability of our textile industry? You saw what happened to Toussard. We would rather live humbly than be starved or killed."

Dominique flinched in her seat next to the Countess at the mention of Bequia.

"We are in a similar position on Iyonola," Martin said, nodding in agreement. "We have some mining, but spice is our staple. We cannot support ourselves without Æcerbot, Kaspan, or Gaul."

Dominique stood. "Are you sure your people would rather live humbly? By humbly, you mean being ground down into an early grave by work and poverty? We have been among the people of each of your respective planets. We have heard their broken songs of struggle. The people want change, and one day, led by you or not, it will happen. Why not trade your fabrics and spice with the other Antilleans in return for their goods and services? Why not set your own prices and have all of the empires pay you fairly? Why not produce more of the necessities your own people need instead of purchasing them from your *master* at the Empire company store? Why do you ship all of your wealth to the empires for a pittance? Only to let them get rich off of your backs and pat you on the head?" Her eyes shone with tears.

The Countess stood next to Dominique and surveyed the worried looks of the leaders' faces. "Invicta does not respect you as people. You will never gain any degree of independence or self-determinism unless you demand it." An uncomfortable silence filled the room that even jovial Davedeo could not break. The Countess could see they would have to drag Æcerbot into negotiations to prove the plan was viable to the Exterran Antilleans, to show them that their lives and work held value and that Æcerbot needed the Antilleans more than the Antilleans needed Æcerbot. The Invictans would continue to starve the Antilleans as long as they believed them to be helpless and dependent. The Empire's hand had to be forced.

"What do you suggest we do?" Martin rubbed his forehead.

"Coordinated labour stoppages. Blockades of major ports, so Æcerbot cargo vessels cannot remove commodities and materials. A general strike if worse comes to worst and they refuse to negotiate," she said unflinchingly.

"Æcerbot will crush we," Ben from Orinoco scoffed.

"They may very well try to," Davedeo said. "But all we are asking for is to be treated as equals and to have some control over our standard of living. We privateers have allies, people on the ground ready to help organize, and we have the capital to support you during work stoppages. We have made inroads with the Kaspans and the Gauls, who will aid us. We won't be completely alone this time. It's now or never." An earnest expression had replaced his usual easy smile.

"All right," Laurette said. The entire room turned to look at her. She squared her shoulders. "Chantimelle will support labour action." She spoke slowly and deliberately as if to mark the gravity of the decision.

"So will we," both Ben and Martin responded almost simultaneously.

"We are united then," the Countess said, relief filling her voice. "We'll discuss the details of our plan in next few meetings."

Æcerbot remained as unyielding as basalt in the interim. The Empire beefed up its transports with military escorts who fired on privateer ships when they drew near in neutral space. While the Æcerbot fleet was large, without a stable supply of iridium alloys to maintain its ships and gates, Æcerbot could not wage war. Neither did it want to for fear of heightening tensions with the Kaspans and Gauls.

"The blockheads aren't budging." Davedeo slapped his palm on the table during one of their frequent talks. "Let's tell the Kaspans and Gauls we'll impede their shipments too if they don't put further pressure on Æcerbot to come to the table. They'll never join forces. They're addicted to getting their commodities cheaply from us. They want Æcerbot to crumble."

The Countess smiled. She poured Davedeo a glass of wine from the silver carafe. "We'll destabilize the peace in all of Exterran space if we have to."

Shipments of all Antillean commodities dwindled. Leadership on Chantimelle, Orinoco, and Iyonola coordinated with one another to send surplus supplies where they were most needed, to help their people weather the economic downturn. Æcerbot could not withstand a long-term shortfall of raw materials. They held out for months. The Countess, Dominique, the privateers, and the Antillean representatives watched reports on the shortages roll in as Æcerbot ships fell into disrepair.

A message came to the Countess via leadership on Icacos, as she was sketching the port from her terrace in the morning sunlight.

It read: *Name your date and place.*

## TEN

# JUSTICE

The Antillean representatives, with the Countess spearheading the meeting, set the summit with Æcerbot to convene on Leeward, a pastoral vacation playground the empires retreated to when discord threatened to shatter Exterran peace. The Leewardian extraplanetary secretary welcomed the Countess and Dominique three days before the meeting and escorted them personally in an enclosed vech to Caldor Estate, just outside the capital, Frontera, where the delegations would parley.

The white stone Caldor manor was bordered by verdant geometric gardens to its left and flanked on the right by a glassy azure lake. The outlying grounds were breathtaking, touching the horizon in every direction. It unsettled the Countess. Tranquil quiet crept into the places inside her where the desolation of the Pit and Bocas comingled. *This is where they've haggled and bartered over rocks with no regard to our fates.* She had to stop herself from blurting this out loud to the secretary.

"I trust you'll find everything satisfactory," the secretary said with a placid smile as he led the Countess and

Dominique into the grand entrance hall. "All manner of dire conflicts have been resolved on Leeward."

"I'm sure we will, thank you." Dominique's charm drew his attention away from the hard set of the Countess's face. She chewed her cheek as the bell men hauled their luggage up to their room.

"Excellent. Staff will be on hand at all times to assist you or to procure anything you should need. I'll leave you both to get settled." The secretary held his right palm up in the Leewardian symbol of farewell and left the staff to show the Countess and Dominique to their suite.

The Countess unpacked while Dominique curled up in a chair in the corner of the room, her face pinched as the muffled quiet of the apartment crowded around them.

"What's wrong?" The Countess paused from hanging a waistcoat in the wardrobe.

Dominique massaged the back of her neck. "How can we trust the Invictans to negotiate in good faith?" Their entire economy is based on exploiting cheap labour to extract raw materials. Why would they loosen their grip on the Antilles when they have nothing to gain?"

The Countess beat back her own nerves, ensuring her voice was as level as slate. "We can't trust them. Tyrants never relinquish power voluntarily; we know that. But the Exterran Antilles are on the verge of solidarity. I can taste it. We've never had *that* before. Toussard tried. His demands were not met and his revolt didn't catch fire past Bequia. None of them could ever come together unanimously to say, 'We refuse to be exploited' in one voice." She dusted off and hung up another waistcoat. "Æcerbot's existence is built on our servitude, our grovelling. They can't function — they do not exist without us. We'll continue to strangle all shipments, all Antillean supplies to Æcerbot. The miners on every territory, on every planet, asteroid, and moon will put down their tools if need be. How will they force us back into subjugation with their stocks of iridium so low? They will have no cloth. They will have no flavour or spice. Invictans will be unable to travel, to eat the foods they love. The cost of their basic necessities will skyrocket. They will negotiate or collapse."

Dominique nodded gravely. Her tone softened. "And what about you?"

"Me?" Surprise made the Countess's voice small.

"Will you rest when this is done? Will you be at peace?" Dominique stood and grabbed her wrist, kissing the branded X upon it.

The Countess's jaw slackened as she stared into the wardrobe. "I will never be at peace again, Dominique."

The Antillean delegation arrived at Caldor two days later. The Countess and Dominique welcomed Laurette of Chantimelle, Martin of Iyonola, and Ben of Orinoco as if they were visiting cousins, along with Phillips from the *Pomerac*. The manor took on an electric but tense mood. The Countess sensed the frisson of apprehension in the air regarding the upcoming negotiations.

"They're nervous," Dominique whispered as they descended the grand staircase on their way to the dining room. The Countess recalled her father's words in the stale hold of the immigrant ship *Zarak*: *Virika means bravery*.

"Fear is bravery's mother," she murmured before they passed through the ceiling-to-floor double doors and into the dining room.

Dominique had curated a menu that referenced dishes from each delegate's culture. Food meant love and care to all Antilleans, and despite their circumstances the Countess and Dominique wanted the representatives to feel at home on Leeward. They wanted them to know they were among friends and family.

The broad table was richly laid with crab soups, pilaus, and callaloos with rice and rotis piled high as accompaniments. The main course was an oil down stew thickened with fresh coconut milk and simmered for hours, which produced a velvety texture and a balanced, full-bodied savoury flavour. After they'd all had their fill, the delegations retired to a drawing room to talk informally.

"Is this the best path for our people? If Æcerbot mining, textiles, or agricultural corps lose controlling interests on our planets, any assistance we'd ever need from Æcerbot in the future would not be guaranteed. We will charge them higher prices, and they will respond by raising the cost of the goods we need from them. We might pay a premium with all of the empires. We'd be unable to support ourselves." Martin of Iyonola said, addressing no one in particular. The question exhumed the anxiety that had been buried beneath the surface of the evening's festivities. The room fractured into heated disparate discussions. The Countess listened to the discourse collapse into calls for easing the demands for Antillean control over industry. Frustration heated her through like embers.

"Why do we continue to ask ourselves how will we survive without them?" Her voice sliced through the talk churning around her. "How do we survive without their abusive paternalism? They have never put the well-being of our people ahead of their limitless greed. We have always, even back on Terra, had to fend for and take care of ourselves. Only we can ensure our well-being. We work the mines and grow the cloth. We know the planets beneath our feet better than any Æcerbot mining corp. We must steer our own destinies."

There was a long pause after she'd finished speaking. Phillips raised his glass.

"Hear, hear," he said. The other delegates raised their glasses but did not echo the toast. The Countess smiled a smile as brittle as her compatriots' resolve. By tomorrow, when the Æcerbot delegation arrived, her people would see that their prosperity depended on each other rather than on the overlords.

In the second silence that followed, Ben of Orinoco addressed the Countess directly. "Why we should trust yuh? Yuh come here wit yuh iridium money and talk of a bettah life out of nowhere. Who are you?"

The Countess swallowed. His voice and accent sounded like her father's. "My family won the lottery and left Orinoco when I was a child. I have not spent my life in the mines, or in the fields. I came of age on Invicta. I grew up following their rules and hating who I am. I was desperate to please them, to be amenable. To work hard. And many of them recognized that and helped me." She exhaled and held up her wrist with the branded X upon it. "But all of that loyalty, all of that devotion meant nothing the moment someone decided I did not deserve my position and status because of who I am and where I was born. My word meant nothing and they threw me in the Pit on Tintaris to die. They will never admit you are good enough, no matter how docile you are. You will always be proving to them that you deserve to live. You must see that you don't need them. Throw off their subsidized protection. You brought them to the table. That has never happened before. Don't take that for granted. They know what you're worth. They would not be here if they didn't. It's time for you to recognize your own value."

She left the drawing room shortly after with Dominique, allowing the Antilleans time in private to mull over what she'd said. She readied for bed straight away, as the Æcerbot representatives were expected at the manor early the following morning. The documents listing their delegation stated that Andilet, now deputy prime minister, along with Lyric, now an attaché, would be among their numbers.

She fell into a sleep as deep as the Pit and found herself locked in her old cell with Captain Whitehall. He was as he'd looked in the hospital: rail thin and corpse-like. On the floor lay Kalima, dead and dressed in a prison uniform.

"Savage," Whitehall raged at her. "You murdered her."

"I didn't," Virika cried. Kalima lifted her head slowly from the concrete floor. She pointed the bleeding end of the stump where Virika had sawed off her hand at Virika.

"You did," Kalima croaked.

She bolted awake drenched in sweat. A sob warped her lips.

"Shhh," Dominique whispered. She kissed Virika's wrist. "They can't hurt you now."

The Antilleans assembled in the grand hall after breakfast to meet the Æcerbot contingent. The junior Invictan officials, dressed in their black tunics, filed in to greet them first. Then followed the senior officials. The Countess begrudgingly shook hands with the minister of defense and the deputy minister of trade. She held her breath, waiting for the faces and names she knew were coming.

Attaché Lyric was announced. A white-hot flash of anger seared through her at the sight of him. His hair was darker than she remembered, his jawline softer. Pent-up rage roiled in her chest. He shook her hand firmly, his familiar daggar stare lurking beneath his civil expression. She stopped herself from smacking him and storming out of the room. The next two delegates passed in a blur as she envisioned smashing Lyric's smug lying face to pieces.

"Minister of Natural Resources Alba Winthrope." The Countess snapped back to attention. Her heart cleaved and quivered. *Alba? She hadn't been on the list.* But there she was, radiant Alba standing in front of the Countess. The shadow of a laugh lurking behind her old lover's lips remained the same. Faint lines bracketed Alba's still full mouth. Her hair was no longer brown but black; her hazel-eyed gaze openly probed the Countess's features.

Sensations flooded back to the Countess as they shook hands. Alba's butter soft skin. The salty taste of her clavicle. Her gasp of ecstasy when Virika's hand eased between her legs. The Countess disintegrated inwardly while she kept her face as blank as a sheet of tin. The two women they'd been in her memory no longer existed. Despite the spark skittering between them in their silent greeting, there was no possibility of rekindling what they'd had. Too much time had passed and they were on opposite sides. The thought of steadfast Dominique waiting for her in their room crushed the Countess's stirring attraction.

Deputy Prime Minister Andilet entered the hall, his face suffused with such abrasive disdain that several of the Antilleans flinched. His grip was like a vise when he shook the Countess's hand. Recognition pierced his expression when he caught her eye. She held his gaze, forcing him to look away first.

After the formal introductions, the Æcerbot contingent were left to settle into the left wing of the manor. The Countess went up to her suite, where she found Dominique engrossed in a book on old Terran customs.

"Alba's here." The Countess collapsed on the bed. Dominique put her book down and angled her head towards the Countess. "She's the Minister of Natural Resources, Dominique. Why would they send both Lyric and Alba, unless they were certain it was me they'd be dealing with? They must have done their own reconnaissance. I saw the look on Andilet's face. He recognized me. Do they think seeing her will throw me off? Or maybe she wanted to see me?"

Dominique came to sit next to her on the bed. "Do you want to see her?" She brushed a wayward lock of hair from the Countess's face.

"No." The Countess exhaled. "That's not true. I do want to see her. I will have to see and talk with her." Her mouth pressed into a tight line. "We're not the same people as we were all those years ago. I want nothing of what she's representing here."

Dominique put her arm around the Countess and kissed her cheek. "Do what you think is best to help our people, but be careful, I can see the effect she has on you."

The Countess, accompanied by Dominique, reluctantly joined the formal dinner that evening. The manor staff had prepared the meal to Æcerbot tastes, and one of the last experiences she wanted to relive was the blandness of the Empire's boiled meat and tubers.

The Antilleans and Invictans sat at opposite ends of the table.

"This whole affair is a waste of money," Deputy Prime Minister Andilet blustered during the second course. "You have self-government."

"We Antilleans have covered most of the expenses for this meeting," Martin pointed out while pushing mushy vegetables about his plate.

"Don't lecture me about finances," Andilet fired back.

"Martin is an expert at balancing budgets," Laurette offered in support, looking askance at her food.

"What do any of you know about managing the economy of an empire on your own?" Andilet thundered at her. "You're amateurs playing at leadership."

The Countess watched Lyric's mouth twitch throughout the exchange as if he were holding himself back from joining. His temper had been hotter than magma when she'd held command over him. His silence now bewildered her.

As the evening dragged on, she tracked a dawning realization among the Antillean leaders: there would be no conciliatory tone offered tomorrow. Not even for the sake of peace and mutual benefit. They'd have to harden their approach or be drubbed by their merciless Invictan counterparts.

Alba caught the Countess's gaze after the meal was over, when the Countess and Dominique stood to leave. Alba flashed her familiar knee-weakening smile. The Countess ignored her and glanced at Dominique before bidding the assembled company goodnight.

The delegates filled into each side of the spacious conference room the following morning. The Antilleans were dressed in brilliant blues, yellows, and reds produced on Chantimelle. The Invictan Æcerbots wore their sombre black tunics. The Countess hung back and sat in the corner of the room. She was not there to negotiate but to observe, to advise, and to threaten if needed. She'd convinced the Antilleans to attempt negotiations, and while the Æcerbots had never acknowledged her, her own people had listened to her and had come to the table with open minds.

The morning's discussions were seized by Æcerbot grievances and straw men. The Invictan officials refused to counter and rejected every Antillean proposal:

"We would like to introduce a standard minimum wage across the Exterran Antilles."

"We will not agree to legislated raises in miners' wages. Corporations must be free to negotiate with their own employees."

"We would like Æcerbot and its companies to set funds aside to assist with mining disasters, pollution, and flooding on agricultural planets."

"Æcerbot will not provide more relief or aid for cleanup or in times of disaster."

"We want to propose changes in laws around profit repatriation so the corporations that dictate our economies contribute fairly to them."

"No. We cannot facilitate the transfer of any further Æcerbot-owned mining or agricultural profits to the Exterran Antilles."

The Countess listened, her resentment compacting into a diamond-sharp point. How had she ever wanted to be one of these pompous Empire puppets who had no desire except further self-advancement and zero recognition of anyone else's humanity? In a repeat performance of the night before, Andilet continued to rant, as inflexible as a block of iron. The defense minister, who was a stranger to the Countess, seethed. Lyric continued to veil his disdain in smooth words and an infuriating calm exterior.

The Antilleans sat blinking in silence as the Invictans stonewalled the discussion. All the while, the Countess squirmed inwardly under Alba's laser-focused scrutiny. When the summit broke for lunch, Alba stood and came towards her. The Countess slipped out of the room before Alba could get close enough to speak.

"How are the negotiations?" Dominique asked while seated for lunch at the table in their room. She'd forgone sitting in on the meeting for fear that her anger would get the better of her.

The Countess laughed, throwing her head back in sardonic mirth. "It's not a negotiation. They refuse to compromise or concede anything, as I predicted." She rubbed her forehead. "They claim we're oppressing *them*."

Dominique poured her a glass of pear juice. "You may have to knock them down several pegs later this afternoon."

The Countess sighed. "I expect I will."

With all reassembled at the table that afternoon, Deputy Prime Minister Andilet stood as if addressing a group of Paria schoolchildren.

"We've played around enough." Exasperation draped the corners of his eyes despite having been in discussion for a mere three hours that day. "You have robbed and looted our ships. Prevented us from maintaining our liveli-hoods. Put us on the brink of war with the Kaspans and the

Gauls. Disrupted the hardworking people of the Empire with food and commodity shortages. You've summoned us, and now you expect us to accept all of your terms. All when you owe your existence to our benevolence. Where would you have been if the Empire hadn't facilitated your ancestors' flight from Terra, where no one wanted you? How dar—"

"Sit down." The Countess's words cracked across the room.

"How dare you treat your benefact—"

"SIT. DOWN." She stood. The table of delegates craned their necks to stare at her. Andilet remained standing, his jaw working.

"No. *You* sit down," he commanded. "You're an escaped convict—"

"You and your Empire are parasites." She spoke over him, her finger jabbing at him like a pick in the air. "The Antilleans owe you nothing. As you have seen, you cannot function without our sweat and blood. You have profited off of us for centuries, going back all the way to Terra." She saw her compatriots nod, spurring her on. "We know our history. It is inscribed in our skins and on our tongues and in the hate for us in your eyes. Now, you will listen, Andilet. We have no masters here. You *will* negotiate. Unlike your Empire, my Antillean compatriots are reasonable. I can't imagine why after you've worked them to death at subsistence wages for corporate profits. Continue to throw these childish tantrums, and not only will we quit this meeting, we will broaden the embargos until you don't have enough raw materials to forge a brick much less get your ships off the ground."

The Countess sat down. Mouths hung open around the brow-beaten room. She gazed at Andilet, despite everyone's focus being on her. He sat, his face ashen. No one had ever spoken to him, or any deputy prime minister, in such a manner. She knew this. His scorn for her had surely escalated to broiling hate.

Lyric cleared his throat. "What was the point we were discussing?"

The meeting resumed. Alba pulled her lips taut and nodded in agreement at the Countess, who licked her lips then returned her concentration to the talks at hand.

Dominique accompanied the Countess to the delegates dinner that evening dressed in a green velvet gown. She sat on the Countess's left, making polite conversation while the Countess, in grey slacks and a waistcoat, poked at her food and blocked out the strained civil talk around her. She did not want to be at this wretched dinner with the people responsible for stealing her life. Andilet glared at her from the other end of the table, which made her want to throw her plate at him. She was only putting in an appearance for Antillean morale.

After a sickly sweet pudding for dessert, the delegates broke off into groups for drinks or to play dominoes. Dominique sat with the minister of trade's secretary while the Countess took her stiff shot of guava rum alone in a club chair. Attaché Lyric was soon looming beside her.

"May I join you, Countess?" He pointed at the chair opposite her.

"You are *free* to sit wherever you wish, Attaché Lyric." She did not give him the consideration of looking him in the eye as she shifted in her chair. He chuckled, which made her want to kick him in the shin.

"How about we step out onto the terrace where we can talk."

She sized him up. He'd remained a wall of muscle even after leaving active service. She'd keep her distance. If he came at her, she would belt him.

"All right." She caught Dominique's eye as she followed him out the terrace doors. She offered a smirk to reassure her she'd be okay.

The evening was warm and the lake glittered like polished platinum in the moonlight. It mesmerized the Countess. She sorely wished Dominique was with her to enjoy it instead of this vile man. The sounds of laughter and dominoes smacking a table in the background were a comfort at least. She wasn't alone here like she'd been on Invicta or in the Pit. She stood across from Lyric and cocked her head, inviting him to speak. His manner became solemn.

"Virika, you have the chance to gain a pard—"

"You may refer to me as the Countess of Sando or Countess." She put her hands on her hips.

"Virika, we know it's you. Cut the act. You look the same." His left eye twitched in spite of the false conciliatory look plastered across his face.

"What act, Attaché Lyric? Your testimony imprisoned Virika Sameroo in a dungeon at the bottom of the Pit on Tintaris. She's dead." She scoffed and looked up at the sky.

"I only told the truth." His voice spiked with indignation. "I saw you keep that coin from the privateer captain."

Miraculously we were able to leave the port unharassed. Then Captain Whitehall ended up ill and dead. The courts agreed. Everyone agreed: you committed treason. And now here you are, the leader of this would-be revolution? A coincidence?"

"You know what happened, Lyric. You heard me say, 'No.' You saw me order the crew to escort the privateer out. You played on the ambiguity of the situation because you were envious Whitehall put me in command over you. You visited the fruit seller and tampered with the packet. I would have died for Whitehall." She pointed at him. "You poisoned him because he saw through you. Verdicts aren't always the truth."

Chin jutted outwards, his calculated demeanour fractured.

"I didn't want you," she continued. "And I, an Antillean woman, was promoted faster than you. It chewed you up inside. You sad, fragile man. It's a story older than time."

"You are an escaped convicted murderer and a traitor to the Æcerbot Empire! Watch how you speak to me, you coolie dog. I'm offering you amnesty and an opportunity to reunite with your mother, which none of my colleagues had originally wanted to offer you."

The mention of her mother rattled the Countess's ire. She held her breath, taking a moment to fortify herself, to quell any questions she had about where her mother was, or whether she was well. This was a ploy. Her mother was the one weak point he could manipulate.

She snorted. "And what do you want me to say, Lyric? Thank you? Thank you for destroying my life for your personal gain while you ask me to betray my people's push for independence? Thank you for asking me to reindenture myself so you'll *allow* me to return to your rotten capital to search for the mother you ripped from me? You and your entire sad delegation are here because I asked you here. This *savage coolie dog* brought your pathetic unfeeling Empire to its knees. You remain here at my pleasure, Lyric, and let me assure you, there has never been anything about you that has pleased me."

"Very well, Countess." His lips were tight. He ducked his head in false reverence. The vein in his temple throbbed. "As you wish." He quitted her and re-entered the manor through the double doors. The Countess moved to the low walls of the terrace to admire the lake and quench her anger.

"It's too lovely a night for such harsh language."

The Countess's heart quaked. She turned. There, splashed in moonlight, was the face from her dreams. Alba. She shivered. It had been her love for her mother and for Alba that kept her alive in the Pit all those bleak years. She could not rush forward and embrace her in the dark. She could not tell her that she'd saved her sanity and her life.

"After being locked at the bottom of the Pit, I never take the stars for granted," she said softly. Alba came closer, so close her lavender scent swept through the Countess, reminding her of lazy afternoons on a blanket in Elmet's centre park and rainy evenings curled up in each other's arms. Her fingers itched to reach out and caress Alba's arm. She refrained. Alba's cheeks flushed.

"You're not the same woman. I was in awe of you as a merchant marine. You were a meteor blazing a trail. You're

147

transcendent here." Alba paused to admire the moon. "I see the respect dripping from the Antillean leaders' faces when you speak. They believe in you. You've gained their trust." She pouted slightly. "I see how Dominique looks at you, too. I envy her." Her voice wavered. The colour in her face deepened. "That used to be me."

"Alba . . ." The Countess searched for words. She would not say sorry, though she *was* bitterly sorry with every sinew of her being. "You seem to have done well for yourself with the time you've had. Minister of natural resources is a prestigious folio. You were a rocket on its way back then as well." She laughed, trying to break the tension. Alba's blush turned splotchy.

"I have." She nodded in agreement. "Perhaps we can take a walk in the gardens the day after tomorrow and I can tell you about it? If it's okay with Dominique, of course."

*I would like that,* was what the Countess wanted to say. "We'll see," was what she said before she bowed sharply and left Alba alone, to rejoin Dominique inside.

There was a knock at the Countess and Dominique's door as they dressed for breakfast the next morning. They locked eyes with one another. Neither had requested anything from the estate's staff. The Countess crossed the room and opened the door.

"A package for you, Countess." A slight young man with black hair handed her a medium-sized white box. Dominique tipped him a sovereign as the Countess went over and put the package on the table in the centre of the room. Eyes narrowed, she stood back to survey it.

"Does it say who sent it?" Dominique asked, coming over to stand beside her.

"Not that I see." The Countess tilted her head. "It has some weight. I'm going to open it."

Dominique shoved herself between the Countess and the box and grabbed the Countess's arm. "No. Let me. What if it's dangerous? They need you at the meetings. You can't be hurt."

The Countess frowned. "Dominique —"

Dominique brushed her aside and removed the cover of the box. She took out a cream envelope addressed in flourishing script to Virika Sameroo. She handed it to the Countess and took out a simple, silver metal vase with a screw top. Virika opened the envelope and unfolded the thick paper inside.

A wounded cry crawled up her throat and forced its way out from her lips. She dropped the letter. Her hands shot up to her mouth and she hunched over as if she'd been punched. Dominique jerked back at the sound. She put the vase on the table, and picked up the paper. She read it out loud:

*Herein are the ashes of Savitri Sameroo. As per her instructions, she was cremated and her remains kept in trust until a relative could be reached to take possession of them.*

Dominique put the letter on the table next to the urn. She reached over and touched Virika's shoulder, but the Countess was petrified stiff. Dominique nudged her gently to the couch. She helped her sit down and sat next to her.

"Virika?" She put her arms around her. "Virika. I love you."

Being called by her name dragged the Countess back to the present. Her chin trembled. She put a hand to her cheek.

"'They've destroyed so much of me. I said, '*No*, no more,' and now they send me my mother's ashes without a word of how she lived or how she died. Yet, *I* am the savage?" She tried to continue, but grief strangled her breath.

"Don't go to the meeting this morning," Dominique said. She cupped the Countess's face in her hands. The Countess shook Dominique's hands away. "This is too much to bear, Virika. Stay here with me. Let yourself feel what you need to feel."

"No." Her voice was failing. "*No*. That's what they want. That's why they did this, to keep me away. They *will* see my face. I have done nothing wrong. They should hide *their* faces. What decent person does this even to their enemy?" She closed her eyes. "I only need a moment."

They took their breakfast in their room. The Countess ate in silence. She worked to recompose herself, to soothe the sorrow that threatened to capsize her. When she'd finished eating, she stood up to get ready for the meeting.

"Will you be okay?" Dominique wrung her hands.

"I want to know who was responsible for sending this to me." The Countess spoke through clenched teeth. "That pig Andilet, after that public dressing down I gave him?"

"Virika, your mother —"

"Do we know it's my mother, Dominique? Can we trust anything they say or do?"

Dominique clasped her hands in front of her as if she were pleading. "Does it matter who did it? They all want to hurt you. Throw you off. They all condone this torture. Each and every one of them."

The Countess mulled over Dominique's point as she adjusted her collar in the mirror. She'd composed her face but could not erase the pain in her eyes.

"Virika and Savitri are dead. Dead people can't be hurt." She saw Dominique grimace behind her in the reflection. She focused on Dominique's face in the mirror. "I can't lose you."

"You won't." Dominique rushed up behind her and kissed her on the neck.

When they parted, the Countess went to the urn on the table and picked it up. Was her mother inside? Either way, Savitri had been lost to the Countess years ago. She placed the cool metal against her forehead as she'd done with the cell door when she'd left Kalima's body behind.

"Success or perish," she said before leaving for the day's meetings.

The Countess sat in her chair in the corner of the meeting room scowling. The Invictans were as eager for her blood as Kaspan wolves. Their stares were the same invisible noose she'd felt in the courtroom so long ago. They knew they'd destroyed her and they were waiting for her to capitulate. She did not mask her contempt for them. Never again would she hide her anger. It danced on her face, a blaze so hot that when she caught the Invictans' glances, they looked away as if they'd been singed. All those years at the academy she'd been force-fed the lie that stoicism was a virtue, that emotion was to be pounded down if one was to command with authority. It was only the Countess and her people who were forbidden to feel. She now knew: anger and spite were swords. She would wield them at every opportunity.

The tone of the negotiations had *miraculously* changed. The summit retrod the proposals the Invictans had dismissed earlier. This time the Empire appeared to want to engage in the work of compromise. Movement had been made on providing a liveable wage to all Antillean workers employed by Æcerbot-owned corporations. They'd agreed to listen to proposals regarding divestment and allowing Antilleans to own and operate their own iridium mining outfits. It had been a productive day.

*Too* productive.

The Antillean delegates met in a private drawing room to confer when the negotiations adjourned for the afternoon. They were puzzled but cautiously hopeful at the day's progress.

"Countess, you've broken through to them." Martin clapped his hands together.

"Yes," added Ben, scratching his head. "But dey change overnight is strange. Yuh don't blast generations of tyranny away with one rebuff."

"Agreed." The Countess pressed her lips together. The spectre of the urn in her room weighed heavy on her mind. "Their complete change of direction is suspicious."

"What could they be planning?" Laurette sat down, her face masked with worry.

"Dey getting us to let we guard down." Ben started pacing the room. "We can't stray. We must keep pushing for dem to allow us control over dee industries we work. At dee very least we need improved workers' rights. Let us remain vigilant."

The Countess put her hands on the table. "Yes. No matter what tactic they try over the next few days, we stand together." The leaders nodded in agreement, committed to their purpose.

That evening after dinner, the Countess watched as Lyric invited Martin out on the terrace, as he'd done with her the night before. Not long after, she watched Lyric storm back inside, his face crimson. She stifled a laugh as she watched Martin return to the room and dust his hands off as if he'd touched something unsanitary.

"Attaché Lyric tried to bribe me into pressuring you all to end the embargo. He said the concessions the Empire had made were fair," Martin reported when the Antilleans reconvened in the private drawing room. Ben let out a heavy sigh.

"Dey tried dee same with me."

"They're searching for the weakest link in our chain," the Countess remarked, shaking her head.

"If we enforce increases in wages and other benefits, why then should we be required to send assistance for disaster relief? Wouldn't you be able to afford to pay for your own disasters in such a situation? You have your own elected representatives. We don't control you." Andilet threw his hands up in the air towards the Countess as he spoke.

"Æcerbot-owned companies control our economies and set prices. You take our resources, use our people, and do next to nothing for our worlds; all of the wealth we create is funnelled back to Invicta," Laurette explained for the second time. "Be honest. Every time we've tried to make our own policies and decisions or tried to provide for ourselves, you've threatened to obliterate our economies, or worse. You denied Toussard's reasonable requests and crushed Bequia for good measure. You are not the patient, benevolent trade partner you claim to be."

The morning's talks had become gridlocked. Æcerbot had hardened its stances again, which left the Antilleans reeling. The Countess opened her mouth, ready to spew venom.

"I think we should take a breather and reconvene tomorrow." Ben pushed his chair back from the table. Heavy murmurs of assent resounded around the room. They were exhausted and getting further way from common ground. All agreed to reassemble around the table the next day.

The Countess took her lunch as usual with Dominique. She then decided to spend the afternoon walking the grounds of Caldera to unwind. Many of the fruit trees were blossoming — the air was sweet with their fragrance. She made a vow to herself: before they left Leeward, she would take her pencils out and sketch the palatial grounds.

"Virika," Alba called from one of the terraces. "May I join you for our aforementioned walk?" Her smile was brilliant even from afar. A tender spot in the Countess's chest throbbed at the sound of Alba saying her name.

"Yes," the Countess said before she could stop herself. Alba hurried down to meet her. The Countess had avoided her during their meetings, but here, standing in front of her in the daylight, she was forced again to consider her long-ago lover. Alba's cheeks were rosy and her expression free of the sadness it carried several evenings ago. Laughter rang in her voice. *Did Alba laugh much during the intervening years?* she thought.

They walked through the thick-hedged grounds in silence, each taking in the splendour of the place. In another life on Invicta, the Countess would have snatched Alba's hand, brought it to her lips, pulled her close, and asked her where she wanted to be kissed that night. She kept a cold arm's length distance between them here.

"I thought I'd never see you again," Alba said when they were out of sight of the manor.

The Countess jammed her fists into her pants pockets. "Do you know what happened to my mother?"

Alba blanched. "The last I knew, she was alive in Paria, where she'd always been." The Countess clicked her tongue.

"And when was that?"

"The week after your sentencing."

The Countess stopped. A sinkhole of anger collapsed inside her. "The last you checked in on my mother was the week after my sentencing a decade ago?"

"How could I go to her?" Alba hunched her shoulders and held out her hands, palms up. "What would the Justice Department have thought if I visited her after you'd been found guilty of treason? My job, my family would have been in danger, too."

The Countess bit the inside of her cheek. Alba's story had a logic to it she could not deny. "You didn't waste the opportunities that were put in front of you in the meantime." She let the bitterness inside her seep into her words.

Alba stopped and faced her. "I would say the same to you. You never sent a message to me after you escaped."

"Do you know what you're suggesting?" she snapped. "Send you a message? Expose myself? You're not serious."

They continued walking, a hard tension solidifying between them. This was a mistake. Recounting their past would only slice open barely healed wounds.

"I'm heading back, Alba." The Countess turned on her heel.

"Virika." Alba grabbed her hand. The Countess's entire body tingled. "Stop this."

"Stop what?" She didn't pull away.

"Stop pretending we mean nothing to each other. We can end this. They'll grant you amnesty, just as Lyric promised the other night on the terrace. End the embargo. Stop threatening a general strike. Tell the Antilleans the compromises we've made are fair. I convinced Andilet you'd compromise if he was more conciliatory. His patience is spent already." Her shoulders dropped. Her eyes shone earnestly.

"Did you know they sent me my mother's ashes this morning?" The Countess's voice smarted with sorrow. "Or was it you who sent them to me?"

"Me?" Alba let go of the Countess and put her hand on her chest. "Virika, you're not making this easy." The words were thick in Alba's throat. Her shoulders stiffened again. "Listen to me. Please."

"Alba. I am not Virika. The woman who loved you is dead. I can't go back with you to your Empire. I cannot betray my people. You said it yourself, they trust me. This is larger than you or me. The Empire has left me for dead too many times. You serve them. I would be a fool to trust them again."

"Virika." She said her name again, this time in the heady way she'd repeated it when they'd been tangled together in bed. A tremor coursed through the Countess. Alba stepped closer. "Do you remember you once said you'd give me your everything?"

The Countess's toes curled at the memory. Alba leaned in, bringing her lips towards the Countess's mouth.

"Lyric came to me after you left my apartment, said he'd end my career if I didn't cooperate with removing you from command. I gave him the coin." Alba's voice pitched higher with her growing desperation. "Andilet will bury me in the Pit if I don't cash in that offer. I can't lose everything I've worked to achieve."

Alba jerked her right arm back. Pressure slammed into the Countess's chest. The Countess stumbled backward. Sharp prickling spread under her collarbone, on the right side of her rib cage. It deepened into a flame of pain burning inside her — it was like nothing she'd experienced before. She put her hand to the spot and pulled it away. It was soaked in blood. Alba stood in front of her, a knife in one hand. Her lips spasmed. The Countess gasped.

"You gave them the coin. They didn't wrench it from you. You locked me away." The Countess stumbled in the direction of the manor. Alba wailed behind her. *Don't let your guard down*, Davedeo had told her. Why had she let herself get so far away from Dominique? Æcerbot was like the cunning vultures of Bocas, circling, probing until they found a weakness to gouge. And she, the Countess, was the weakness. "Why?" she choked out between gasps of pain. "Did you ever love me?"

"Yes," Alba sobbed. "I loved you. But love isn't enough." Her words amalgamated with the rush of blood in the Countess's ears and the visceral pulsing in her chest. The Countess stumbled forward. Dizziness descended on her. She neared the terrace where Alba had run out to her. Ben and a secretary from Chantimelle were chatting there. She tripped and cried out. Ben shouted and rushed over to her.

Kalima's voice filled her head: *Perhaps, I am going home after wandering the sea.*

Everything went black.

The secretary from Chantimelle ran into the manor to alert its staff to the Countess's injury. Dominique bolted from the terrace and shoved everyone huddled around the Countess aside. She dropped to her knees and cradled the Countess's head in her lap.

"No." She sobbed and kissed the brand on the Countess's wrist.

"There's nothing I can do for her," the pallid-faced medic pronounced not long after he arrived. The Antilleans encircled the Countess, their heads bowed. Tears gushed openly. They would not hide or wipe them away. Dominique remained on her knees. The Æcerbot contingent watched from the terrace. Alba was among them, spattered in the Countess's blood.

"The Antillean representatives suspend all negotiations with the Æcerbot Empire and its representatives," Dominique announced when the delegations met the next morning.

"What you've done is unconscionable," Laurette continued after her, glaring in contempt at the Invictans across the table. "It is a grave crime. We have negotiated peacefully and in good faith for a fair deal that would be to our mutual benefit. We will *not* stand by while you murder our people in cold bold for your own financial gain." She, Martin, and Ben turned their backs on the Invictans before filing out of the room.

"It was self-defence," Alba reported when questioned. As both delegations had met under diplomatic circumstances, under Leewardian law, she was granted immunity. The Invictans, Andilet, Lyric, and Alba, along with their retinues, were permitted to leave Leeward undeterred days later.

Davedeo and the crew of the *Pomerac*, along with the privateer captains on word from Dominique, Laurette, and the others, strengthened the embargo and blamed Æcerbot for delayed shipments to the Kaspans and Gauls, pushing them into open hostilities with the Æcerbot Empire.

"We call on dee Exterran Antilles to have no dealings with Æcerbot." Ben from Orinoco, backed by the other leaders, delivered a prepared speech broadcast across their star system. "Æcerbot has murdered dee Countess who fought to improve we futures during negotiations. Invicta has ground we lives and bodies to dust while dey prospered. Dey have not agreed to work towards we mutual economic benefit or even raise we wages. We must cast off dese oppressors. We must come together as one, if we are to have a future as a people. We will block iridium, cloth, spice, and other exports bound for Æcerbot. Æcerbot Corp-owned property will be seized for we own benefit. We will strengthen our ties with dee Kaspan and Gauls, who have been willing to work with we."

"We'll negotiate," the Æcerbots begged as their food and supply chains began to collapse. They tried reaching out to the Kaspans and Gauls to ask them to act as intermediaries. The new Antillean federation, united after the Countess's death responded:

*The United Federation of the Antilles does not negotiate with tyrants and murderers.*

The Countess was cremated on a pyre like her mother and father before her, at dawn on the fifth day following her death. The ceremony was private, with only Dominique and the crew of the *Pomerac*, who were the Countess's only family, in attendance.

"I don't want a lavish send-off when I die," the Countess had told Dominique. "We could never have brought the

Antilleans together without Kalima's sacrifice, without the sacrifice of every unknown miner and Antillean before me whose name will never be recorded in the history books. Who will mark the end of my Tanager's life at the bottom of the Pit?"

Dominique visited Orinoco months later, when she found the strength. The Countess's name echoed in the songs of the market women in Sando. She'd possessed their spirits, despite wanting to fade from history. Dominique piloted a PIP to Bequia and booked into the same hotel she and Virika had stayed at together while on their way to Bocas. The streets of Nova had revived with the fever of self-determination and the spirit of Toussard's revolution. A crowd filled the broken capital's square to listen to Dominique speak at a rally championing the Federation's cause.

They met her with open hearts.

She addressed them on a rain-drenched morning. "Fear is bravery's mother. There will be more cruel hardship ahead. There will be shortages. They will try to starve and kill us. But we will be free. We will rebuild. Do not stifle your anger or hide your broken hearts. Use them. Channel them into our cause."

They roared and chanted Toussard's name in the packed streets.

Dominique then left for Bocas alone, haunted by the knowledge that this was only the beginning of their fight. Æcerbot would never relinquish its wealth and power quietly. The cause had taken her father's life, and the Countess's. More innocent people would be killed, more children orphaned. Invicta would set blood as the price of freedom.

The lonely dwarf planet Bocas hung before her, shining like an emerald and sapphire pendant in the darkness. Using the PIP's remote arms, Dominique scattered the Countess's ashes, along with her mother's, among Bocas's alabaster ring. The dust dispersed across her field of vision, intermingling with the bones that encircled the planet. The hum that filled Bocas's caves vibrated the cockpit. It echoed in her head, morphing into Virika's determined voice.

"Success or perish," Dominique said through her tears, in unison with Virika. "Success or perish."

THE END

# ACKNOWLEDGEMENTS

Thanks to Michael Curry, my agent, who was the first person to read *Countess* and who believed in it from day one. Your constant support has meant a lot to me. To Jen Albert my editor, it was incredible working with you. You understood the heart of the book and helped me tell the story I wanted to tell. You've taught me so much. I am a better writer because of you. Thank you also to the ECW team for your work and support. You've all been lovely.

To my family, friends and those who helped me throughout this process, you have my profound gratitude. I was in a very, very dark place when I wrote this novella and you helped me crawl out of it. Indomitable hope — that's what you gave me. I wouldn't be anywhere without you. Much love.

SUZAN PALUMBO is a Trinidadian-Canadian dark speculative fiction writer and editor. Her short stories have been nominated for the Nebula, Aurora, and World Fantasy Awards. Her debut dark fantasy/horror short story collection, *Skin Thief: Stories*, is out now from Neon Hemlock. She lives in Brampton, Ontario.

**Entertainment. Writing. Culture.** ────────────

ECW is a proudly independent, Canadian-owned book publisher. We know great writing can improve people's lives, and we're passionate about sharing original, exciting, and insightful writing across genres.

──────────────── **Thanks for reading along!**

We want our books not just to sustain our imaginations, but to help construct a healthier, more just world, and so we've become a certified B Corporation, meaning we meet a high standard of social and environmental responsibility — and we're going to keep aiming higher. We believe books can drive change, but the way we make them can too.

Being a B Corp means that the act of publishing this book should be a force for good – for the planet, for our communities, and for the people that worked to make this book. For example, everyone who worked on this book was paid at least a living wage. You can learn more at the Ontario Living Wage Network.

This book is also available as a Global Certified Accessible™ (GCA) ebook. ECW Press's ebooks are screen reader friendly and are built to meet the needs of those who are unable to read standard print due to blindness, low vision, dyslexia, or a physical disability.

The interior of this book is printed on Sustana EnviroBook™, which is made from 100% recycled fibres and processed chlorine-free.

ECW's office is situated on land that was the traditional territory of many nations including the Wendat, the Anishnaabeg, Haudenosaunee, Chippewa, Métis, and current treaty holders the Mississaugas of the Credit. In the 1880s, the land was developed as part of a growing community around St. Matthew's Anglican and other churches. Starting in the 1950s, our neighbourhood was transformed by immigrants fleeing the Vietnam War and Chinese Canadians dispossessed by the building of Nathan Phillips Square and the subsequent rise in real estate value in other Chinatowns. We are grateful to those who cared for the land before us and are proud to be working amidst this mix of cultures.

**ecwpress.com**